Something thudd

A hush fell over the ent

A moment later, Zeke's brother pounded at the door.

Zeke rushed over, Molly on his heels. He looked out and saw his brother holding the body of the officer who'd been guarding the *haus*. With an exclamation, he threw the door wide open, then helped Micah bring the man inside, vaguely aware that Molly was ordering the *kinder* to go into the other room.

Blood was spreading over the man's shirt. But he was breathing.

"Call 911!" Micah barked.

Molly. Where was Molly?

Spinning around, Zeke spotted her standing with her back to the open door, her hands covering her mouth. Behind her, a shadow moved. He didn't even think. Diving toward her, he knocked her out of the doorway. They rolled onto the floor.

A knife whizzed into the room, making a solid thunk as it hit the wall, vibrating with the force of impact.

Had he not pushed her out of its path, it would have sunk deep into her back.

Whoever had been searching for her knew where she lived.

Dana R. Lynn grew up in Illinois. She met her husband at a wedding and told her parents she'd met the man she was going to marry. Nineteen months later, they were married. Today, they live in rural Pennsylvania with their three children and a variety of animals. In addition to writing, she works as a teacher for the deaf and hard of hearing, and is active in her church.

Books by Dana R. Lynn

Love Inspired Suspense

Amish Country Justice

Plain Target
Plain Retribution
Amish Christmas Abduction
Amish Country Ambush
Amish Christmas Emergency
Guarding the Amish Midwife
Hidden in Amish Country
Plain Refuge
Deadly Amish Reunion
Amish Country Threats
Covert Amish Investigation
Amish Christmas Escape
Amish Cradle Conspiracy
Her Secret Amish Past
Crime Scene Witness
Hidden Amish Target

Visit the Author Profile page at LoveInspired.com for more titles.

HIDDEN AMISH TARGET

DANA R. LYNN

LOVE INSPIRED SUSPENSE
INSPIRATIONAL ROMANCE

LOVE INSPIRED® SUSPENSE
INSPIRATIONAL ROMANCE

ISBN-13: 978-1-335-59895-0

Hidden Amish Target

Recycling programs
for this product may
not exist in your area.

For questions and comments about the quality of this book, please contact us
at CustomerService@Harlequin.com.

Love Inspired
22 Adelaide St. West, 41st Floor
Toronto, Ontario M5H 4E3, Canada
www.LoveInspired.com

Printed in U.S.A.

And he said to them all, If any man will come after me, let him deny himself, and take up his cross daily, and follow me.
—*Luke* 9:23

To my children: Rachael, Bradley and Gregory. I'm so proud of the adults you've become. I'm blessed to be your mom.

Acknowledgments:

Each book I write is an adventure with unique ups and downs. I'm so grateful for all the support during the journey.

Thanks to my husband, Brad, and my children. I appreciate your flexibility when my book took over the dining room table.

Amy and Dee, my best friends. I don't know how I'd do it without our coffee dates.

To the Suspense Squad. You ladies have enriched my life and my writing.

To my many writing friends who have laughed, cried and prayed with me throughout this journey, I love you all!

To my launch team, you ladies amaze me with your generous spirits and loving natures. A special thanks to Caron Tweet, a launch team member and friend who is now with Jesus. I will miss you.

Thank you to my editor, Tina James, and my agent, Tamela Hancock Murray. I am so honored to work with you.

Especially, to my Lord Jesus Christ. I pray that my words bring You glory. Help me always walk in Your ways.

ONE

"Are you sure you won't need a ride back?"

Molly Schultz forced herself to smile at her friend, Adele King. They'd been friends for years, although they didn't see each other as much as they used to since the accident that had changed Molly's life a little over a year ago. Adele had been there whenever she needed her, though.

Molly opened the door before swinging down from the front bench of the buggy. She caught herself before her feet stumbled when they landed on the edge of the pothole in the paved road. Hot pain shot up her right leg, the one that had been broken in two places. It healed over time, but occasionally let her know it wasn't perfect anymore. It was a toss-up whether her clumsiness was because of exhaustion, the late-morning July heat or the condition of the roads in Sutter Springs, Ohio. Straightening, she thought she'd saved her dignity quick enough, until a wave of quiet laughter hit her ears. Making a silly face, she wiggled her fingers at the two *kinder* giggling inside. They laughed harder, their small shoulders shaking. This time, when she smiled, it was genuine. She loved *kinder*. If only…

She pushed the thought away, refusing to allow discontent to settle in her soul. She was blessed. She had to remember that. She could have lost so much more when a drunk driver has crashed into a group of Amish leaving a church gathering thirteen months ago, killing eight people and injuring five more. She still had *Mamm* and her sisters. What she had lost, however, continued to haunt her, following her into nightmares that forced her to relive the horror until she woke up sobbing in her pillow.

The dreams were less frequent now, but she doubted they'd ever leave completely.

Her mother had encouraged her to write and offer forgiveness to the young man who'd caused the trauma with his poor choices. She hadn't done that yet. How could she offer forgiveness? It would be a lie. Collin Vincent had walked away from the accident without a scratch. He'd lost his driver's license and had been sentenced to five years in prison. He'd be released and free to live his life in four years, but her *daed* and Aaron would still be dead.

"Molly?"

She blinked, flushing. She'd gotten so caught up in her thoughts she'd forgotten Adele was waiting. She blocked the memory of that infamous day from her mind and smiled again. Dear Adele would do anything to help, but she had her own family and her work at her father's business, the Plain and Simple Bed and Breakfast.

"*Ja*, I'm sure I don't need a ride back. This is the only *haus* I have to clean today, and it's a wonderful *gut* day to walk, *ja*? I'm only a mile from home. I'll finish here by one and get home by two." She pulled her cleaning bucket from the floor of the buggy and backed away to escape the dust kicked up by the mare's prancing hooves. She didn't want to think about walking a mile with her leg still aching. Before the accident, that wouldn't have fazed her. "*Denke* for the ride."

"Anytime, Molly. I'll see you in church on Sunday." Adele grasped the reins firmly in both hands.

Molly winced, and not in pain. Church. She'd have to smile at people who muttered platitudes and urged forgiveness. That is what *Gott* wanted. It just wasn't in her yet. Still, Adele didn't need to know how far she'd fallen. She raised her hand. "*Ja.* See you Sunday."

Adele flicked the reins, setting the impatient mare off at an easy trot. Molly backed up again and waved to the sweet *kinder* peering out the window. When the buggy turned at the corner and vanished from view, she sighed. The past year had changed her life in so many ways. Her father and her fiancé were dead, her only brother was still in a coma and her mother was paralyzed. Her two youngest sisters were still in school, leaving Molly and her sixteen-year-old sister, Abigail, to shoulder most of the chores and pay the bills.

Trudging up the driveway, Molly was nearly to the back door when she noticed the car was gone. She slowed, then halted. Nancy Stevens's Buick was normally sitting there when she arrived. After a moment, Molly bit her lip. What should she do? She'd never cleaned the *haus* before when no one was home. It seemed wrong to enter someone's home when they weren't there. However, Nancy Stevens and her husband, Frank, were very busy people. Which was why Nancy had given Molly a *haus* key a few weeks after she'd hired her to clean every Tuesday morning. Molly was an hour later than usual today, due to a mess her sister Rhoda had made while trying to cook breakfast. She'd spent a precious half hour trying to soothe the distraught teenager while getting the kitchen back into order. She got way behind schedule, but she didn't have a specific time she needed to arrive by. Nancy had probably been too busy to wait to let her in. Shaking herself out of the ridiculous feeling of unease crawling over her skin, she turned her gaze away from the empty driveway and plodded around to the back door.

Unlocking the door, she entered the large airy kitchen and left her boots on the linoleum floor. Shutting the door behind her so the airconditioning wouldn't escape, she padded in her stockinged feet through the kitchen, where she filled her bucket with water and soap. Then she headed through the dining room and climbed the stairs to the second floor, lugging her bucket all the way. For some reason, Nancy and Frank hadn't put air conditioners in the upstairs of the *haus*. That was one reason she always started at the top and worked her way down. It would be awful working in the sweltering second floor later in the day when the heat rose. As it was, sweat was already gathering at her collar and on her back. Partway up the steps, the bucket bumped into her knee, splashing soapy water on her rose-colored dress. She grimaced. Now she'd be hot, sticky and wet while she cleaned.

An hour into her cleaning, a car pulled into the driveway. Assuming Nancy had returned, Molly continued working. She tuned out any sounds from downstairs while she dusted.

Until the shouting began.

Freezing, her dusting rag clenched in her hand, she listened. She'd never heard the first voice before. It was deep. Anger seethed in the rich tones. She shivered. There was something menacing about the man's tone. Her stomach clenched.

A younger voice entered the fray. She knew that one. Terry, the Stevenses' only son. He was a handsome young man with a smooth smile and a reckless air. He was a little younger than her own twenty-three years, maybe around twenty, and held the mistaken belief that he was charming. Even though he knew she was Amish, he insisted on flirting with her anytime they happened to be in the same room. She'd never trusted him. His parents considered him the perfect son, but she always felt something dark stared at her from behind his eyes and brilliant smile.

The shouting grew louder. She couldn't understand the words, but she wasn't about to stick around and be a witness to family drama. She'd explain to Nancy later why the cleaning hadn't been completed. She carried the bucket to the upstairs bathroom and dumped the dirty water in the sink.

The back door slammed. Heels clicked across the kitchen floor. "Terry? What's going on?"

Nancy was home. Relieved, Molly's shoulders relaxed. When the shouting didn't cease, she continued gathering her cleaning supplies, shoving the rags into a grocery store bag and tucking it under her arm. Grabbing her bucket, Molly fled down the stairs, sneaking like a mouse trying to outsmart a barn cat. Thankfully, the stairs were carpeted. She arrived at the back door and shoved her feet into her boots.

The shouting grew frantic.

"Wait!" Nancy and Terry both screamed.

A single gunshot blasted.

Molly dropped her bucket and the bag, sending rags and cleaning supplies clattering across the white-and-yellow linoleum kitchen floor, making more noise than a flock of riled-up guinea hens. She fumbled with the back door, praying to escape before anyone found and caught her.

She had never been in such a situation before where she could feel danger stalking her. She needed to get out, get help. A gunshot in a house meant something bad was happening.

There was a thud in the back of the *haus*, followed by loud footsteps tromping to the closed doorway of the den. Whoever had fired that shot might be heading her way.

Now!

Finally pulling the door open, Molly threw herself out of the *haus* and raced down the doorway, ignoring the pain in her weak leg. The door had barely clicked shut when it burst open again.

"You!" the angry voice thundered behind her. It was the man who'd been shouting at Terry. Had he shot Terry or Nancy? How close was he? She didn't take the time to look over her shoulder. A gun barked and a bullet thunked into a tree a foot away from her. She'd been right to leave. She had to find someone who could help.

Leaning forward, she pumped her arms and put on another burst of speed. She rounded the corner of the *haus* and ran down the driveway. Nancy's Buick was parked in front of the left garage door. An unfamiliar yellow car blocked the other bay.

It had to belong to the man chasing her.

The man with the gun yelled at her again and pounded after her. His footsteps clomped nearer with every passing second.

He's going to catch me.

She hit the pavement and tore off down the street, sobbing when she hit a small pile of gravel and her ankle twisted. She couldn't stop. She continued running, the sore ankle causing her to limp and slowing her pace.

"Hey!" She turned her head. Terry Stevens ran out and tackled the man. They both went down in a pile of fists and fast punches on the side of the road.

Molly slowed. She wanted to keep running, but Terry could be in trouble. The stranger lifted his head and glared at her through angry dark eyes. Terry's fist collided with his face. With a grunt, the man refocused on him.

Her eyes met Terry's for a second.

"Go!" he screamed.

She ran, veering off the road and smashing into the trees, trespassing across the backyards of the *hauser* on the next street over. She hadn't gone far before she heard another gunshot. Her blood turned to ice in her veins. She knew what had happened.

Nancy and Terry had both been shot. She had to somehow escape and inform the police. But how?

She didn't pause until she was three blocks over in a more rural area where the occasional barn dotted the landscape. Bending at the waist, she opened her mouth and sucked in huge gulps of air. Pressing her hand against the ache in her side, she tried to plan.

Someone thrashing through the trees nearby informed her that her respite was over. But if she ran, there was no way to hide. He had a gun. If he shot now, here on the open street, anyone passing by could be harmed.

Out of options, she ran to the left and dropped down behind a white van, trembling, the blood pounding in her ears.

Please, Lord, don't let him see me.

The front driver's side of the van opened. She held her breath.

"I can only talk for a few minutes. I'm on a job…" a male voice said, clearly speaking into a phone, accompanied by the sound of shoes scuffing against the black tar driveway. Both sounds drifted away from the van. She inched toward the end of the van and peered around. The driver continued ambling toward the road, his back facing her.

A car crawled past him. It was the one that had been at the Stevenses' *haus*. She jerked her head back behind the cover of the van, praying fervently. If he'd glimpsed her, she was as good as dead.

The vehicle continued past. The painful breath she'd been holding released in a hard exhale. She couldn't walk away. Not when he was so close. Would he continue moving away, or would he circle back? Her options were gone.

Unless…

She stood up behind the van before she could talk herself out of it and opened the left door. It was full of farrier tools. Scrambling up inside, she closed the door, sealing her fate. Then she wedged herself into the right corner, directly behind where the driver would be sitting.

It was a foolish thing to do. She had trapped herself inside. The owner would be furious. But if she made it back to his workshop, she'd be alive, she'd be able to get help for the Stevenses and maybe he'd be willing to let her explain.

It was the only choice she could make with a killer searching for her. A killer who had seen her face.

Zeke Bender signed the handwritten invoice on his clipboard. He carefully separated the white customer copy from the triplicate form and handed it to the stable manager, taking the accordion-style file folder from under his arm and stuffing the pink and yellow carbon copies inside under his tab for Tuesday.

"Thanks, Zeke." Chuck looked over the invoice, nodded, then pocketed it. "Great work, as usual. You're the only farrier I trust to shoe my horses."

"You're welcome. I'd not use the paint mare for lessons for the next week. She's not used to wearing shoes yet. She needs a few days to adjust."

"I don't have her slated to be put on the lesson schedule until the beginning of August, so we're good."

Zeke shook hands with Chuck. "I'll be back in a week to check on her, say?"

"That'll work. Whenever you show up, someone will be around."

Zeke nodded, then turned to get into the van he'd hired for his appointments this week. The wagon he kept especially for his business was out of commission. He had built it himself. Behind its black cab, there was a flatbed surrounded on the sides by straights slats of black metal. Honestly, to him it resembled an *Englisch* pickup truck, just towed by a horse. Unfortunately, during a storm a few months ago, a tree had fallen on it and damaged several of the metal slats and bent the rear wheel axles. He would fix it as soon as he had the free time, but he had a full schedule at the moment.

Until then, he needed to rely on drivers.

The one he hired was currently AWOL, as Micah would say. Shaking his head, he settled into his seat to wait for Neil to show up, smiling slightly as he imagined his brother's reaction to him using an *Englisch* acronym for "absent without official leave." He'd learned several interesting terms from his older brother, an ex-Amish US deputy marshal.

The door opened, breaking into his thoughts. Neil hopped behind the wheel and pulled his seat belt into place.

"Sorry, Zeke." The engine roared to life. Zeke winced. Neil should check out the muffler. The van sounded like a small airplane. "I had a call I had to take from my mom."

Zeke nodded. One should never ignore their mothers. "It's *gut*. This is my last appointment for the day. I can do the rest of my work from home."

Neil shifted the van in Drive. He waited for an oncoming car to pass. "That dude needs to use his gas pedal. The speed limit is forty-five on this road, not five."

Zeke narrowed his eyes, frowning as he watched the progress of the yellow car in question. "That's the second time he's driven past in the last ten minutes. I wonder if he's lost."

A snort left Neil. "If he has a phone, he's got GPS."

Not knowledgeable regarding either phones or GPS systems, Zeke refrained from commenting. Something about the man bothered him. He didn't scour the mailbox as if he were searching for an address. Rather, his gaze scanned the surrounding yard and trees, squinting as if he were trying to peer deep into the barns populating the stable grounds and beyond.

He shifted, uneasy until the car moved on. As an afterthought, he focused on the license plate, attempting to memorize it, feeling foolish. Still, he didn't look away.

The offending vehicle turned and drove out of sight. Neil pulled out on the road, heading in the opposite direction. Zeke faced the front of the van, but he couldn't get that man's angry expression out of his mind.

It was almost two when they arrived at his property. They pulled past the first building. At one time, another *haus* had stood there and he'd lived in it with his wife, Iris. After she'd died, he'd donated the structure to the local fire department to use for a rescue drill. After the *haus* had burned down, the Amish community had rallied around and built a new one for him. He couldn't bring himself to live there, even though it was a different building. With his brothers' help, he'd erected a second *haus*, where he lived alone. In the first one, he had knocked down many of the walls and made it his workshop.

Zeke dismounted from the van and moved to the back. He opened the left door and grabbed the first batch of tools and supplies.

"Hey, I can help you." Neil approached around the corner.

"*Denke.* If you can put these into the barn along the wall, that would help."

He passed the bundle to his unexpected assistant, then opened the other door. He reached for the next bundle of tools.

"Zeke!" a voice hissed from inside the van.

He dropped the tool bucket he'd pulled out. Looking inside, he didn't see anyone. "Hello?"

Had he imagined the voice calling his name?

"Zeke," the voice whispered again. "I'm stuck in the corner."

Leaning forward, a pair of blue eyes stared up at him. Zeke blinked, sure he was seeing things. When he glanced a second time, the young woman was still there, crouched behind the tools that had shifted during the short drive and caged her in. By the way she was holding her arms to protect her head, he suspected she'd been hurt a little. There wasn't a way to know how much until he got her out of the van.

He turned toward the barn to call Neil and ask for assistance.

"Wait!"

He turned his gaze to the woman tucked into the van. She looked up, her expression pleading. His mouth dropped open when he realized he knew her.

Molly Schultz. It had been quite some time since he'd seen her, but he'd know those blue eyes anywhere. He'd also recognized the small scar along her jawline, just below her right ear. He was there when she'd earned that by falling out of a tree at the age of four.

His family and her family had belonged to the same church district when they were *younger*. In fact, her older brother, Caleb, had been his best friend. When he was twelve and Caleb was nine, the district had reached forty families, which was too large, and had split into two districts. Molly was nearly five at the time. Although the Bender and Schultz families still saw each other, the instances he and Caleb hung out together decreased as they each began to attend church events in their own district.

"Molly."

She made a shushing noise. "Please. Zeke, people need help. And I'm in danger. No one can know where I am."

He opened his mouth to ask for more details. Hearing footsteps, he paused. Although he didn't know what kind of trouble she was in, he'd respect her wish for privacy until he knew more. He had to hurry if he was going to keep her presence a secret. "Quick."

He shoved the tools out of the way. Reaching closer, he leaned against the bumper and held out a hand to her. She surged forward, grabbing his hand and awkwardly stepping over the equipment littering the back of the vehicle, placing her feet in the empty spaces. She let go of his hand and leaped out of the van, wobbling slightly as she landed on her feet. He recalled hearing that she'd been injured in the accident that had killed her *daed* and put Caleb in a coma. Reaching out an arm, he steadied her briefly.

She shook off his arm and dashed to the left side of the van. He saw her crouch low. That wouldn't work for long. Suddenly, he remembered the other driver searching for something. Surely not Molly? He couldn't shake the idea. Something bad had to have happened for brave Molly Schultz to take refuge in a strange van.

Neil popped around the right side, whistling. He eyed the tools cluttering the ground. "I wondered what had kept you. Need any help picking those up?"

He couldn't have Neil stepping any closer to her hiding spot. As much as he himself trusted Neil, Zeke knew Molly was afraid, and he'd respect that. He grabbed the first item he found and thrust it at Neil.

"*Nee.* If you take this—" he glanced to see what he'd handed him "—crate of horseshoes and nails, I'll be able to get the rest, *ja*?"

"Will do." Neil lifted the crate to his shoulder like a waiter with a tray full of dishes and started for the barn.

Zeke poked his head around the van. Molly's eyes were wide and panicked, her face ashen. He kept his voice low.

"While he's gone, my workshop is there." He pointed to the building. "It's open. Hide in there until I can come and tell you it's safe."

She ran for the workshop, running hunched over in an attempt to make herself small and unnoticeable. Which would be difficult.

Molly was taller than most women he knew. Maybe five foot nine. She was only an inch or so shorter than he was.

He needed to hurry so Neil could leave. Curiosity burned inside him. He hadn't been really intrigued by anything since his wife died nearly a year and a half ago. At thirty-one, he'd been living day by day, merely trying to get through from dawn until he could sleep and close out the world again. This new sense of curiosity disturbed him. The last thing he wanted was to open himself up for more pain and betrayal. He figured he'd had enough of that to last the rest of his life.

Hefting the rest of the tools, he strode to the barn. Normally, he'd store them in his workshop, but he didn't want Neil to enter and find Molly hiding there before he had an opportunity to question her.

"Is that the rest of it?" Neil brushed his hands off.

"*Ja*. It went fast, with you helping me. I appreciate your generosity."

Neil ducked his head, dodging his gaze. He shoved his hands into his pockets. "Well, to be truthful, I wasn't being that generous. My mom needs me at home, so I thought I'd hurry things along." He held up both hands. "Not that I mind helping. You're paying me well. If you need me to stay…"

Zeke didn't roll his eyes, but it was a close call. "*Nee*, you go home. Help your mother. I have work to do here."

"Great." Neil speed walked toward his van. About halfway between the barn and the van, he turned and walked backward. "Same time tomorrow?"

"*Ja*. Same time."

Relief crossed the young man's face. Clearly, he worried that he'd lost the job due to his attitude. But Zeke had no problem with him leaving in a hurry. Family came before business. In fact, it worked in his favor not to have anyone else hanging around.

Standing in the entranceway, he remained in that spot for a moment or two after Neil was gone. What could have possibly happened to Molly? He hadn't seen her for a while. Even before the accident, his family and hers hadn't crossed paths much. He'd still seen Caleb a few times a year, but other than that, he'd become deeply immersed in his business and his own life. And after Iris had died, he'd lost all interest in socializing with anyone, whether they were old friends or new.

His thoughts zeroed in on Molly. She'd never been the type to hide or back away from confrontation. Micah would have described her as a "take a bull by the horns kind of girl." She'd always been opinionated and feisty. He recalled some of the arguments he'd heard between Molly and Caleb growing up. More often than not, they ended with Caleb throwing up his hands and walking away, leaving Molly the undeclared victor.

That strong woman had been hunched over and huddled in the back of the van like a victim. That didn't sit right with him. Not at all. No one should have to cower like that. Especially not brave young women who seized every day with zest and joy.

There'd been no joy in her gaze when it had collided with his.

Shutting the door behind him, he strode to the workshop, determined to uncover the mystery of what had changed and put that look of terror in her fine blue eyes.

TWO

What had she done?

Molly paced back and forth between the main worktable and the wall, avoiding walking in front of the windows. She couldn't stop shaking. It was as if her body was unraveling from the inside out.

Molly crossed her arms around her torso, holding herself together. She'd been so relieved when Zeke had first opened the van door and recognized her. Seeing a familiar face had done much to ease her terror.

But now, she regretted her impulse. The memory of the gunshots and Nancy's scream was seared into her mind. Molly flinched. Logically, she knew running was the correct choice to make. Only then could she somehow seek help for them. If she'd stayed, she'd be dead, even now. Yet, her soul recoiled at her actions. She felt as if she'd abandoned them to their fate. Were either of them still alive?

Stopping in the middle of the floor, she bowed her head. But her mind remained blank. It had been so long since she'd communicated regularly with *Gott*. Even her prayer for Him to keep her family safe had been more of a reflex than a conscious act of will. Now that she wanted to pray, needed to open her heart to *Gott*, there was nothing there.

Groaning deep in her throat, she began pacing again. Her leg ached but moving helped her think. Besides, if she stood still too long the limb would become stiff. Rubbing her hands over her face, she tried to think of her next move. Obviously, the *Englisch* law needed to be alerted.

On her own, she didn't see how that would happen. Her only hope was Zeke. How much had he changed since she'd last seen him? He'd already assisted her, without knowing what she faced. Maybe so he'd be willing to help again.

Growing up, she'd always liked Zeke. Where most of the older boys her brother had hung out with had been louder and talked fast, Zeke had been quiet. Not shy or awkward, just thoughtful. He kept to himself, but she'd seen him show compassion to the younger *kinder* or stop to assist an elder in their church without being asked. And he never seemed to expect acknowledgment. It was simply who he was. Had the trials in his life damaged the strong, heroic heart she'd so admired?

Zeke had that bruised look of trauma stamped on his face and in the stiff manner of his shoulders. She'd heard his wife had died, although she didn't know all the details. Now she was bringing the chaos and horror of what she'd seen to his *haus*, the one place he should be able to relax. If it weren't for the sake of Nancy and Terry, she'd leave. But she'd never be able to live with herself if she discovered they'd been alive, but her inaction had caused them to die before help could arrive.

Nor would she ever forget the face of the man who had come after her, a hunger for her death glinting in his cold eyes.

Although she liked to solve her problems and hated to ask anyone for assistance, this was one time she was out of her depth. She couldn't find help on her own. Not with their killer out there, searching for her. But she hated to embroil Zeke in more drama.

She pivoted and took two more steps, then stopped, horror freezing her in place. Her family. What if this killer learned who she was and went after her family? How thoughtless was she that she'd never thought of all the consequences of her actions?

Spinning, she lurched toward the door, nearly falling out and into Zeke's arms as he pulled it open from the outside.

"Molly! What's wrong?" Concern throbbed in his deep, calm voice.

"I have to go," she sobbed, frantic. "My *mamm* and my sisters, they're in danger!"

He came into the room slowly, his unwavering gaze resting on her. His brow furrowed. The door closed behind him, sealing them in the workshop together. For a moment, silence reigned, broken only by a single sobbing breath she released.

She stopped moving in front of him, suppressing the urge to shove him out of the way and run out the door. What would be the use? Covering her face, she slumped against the wall, sliding down until she was sitting on the floor, her grief and fear clouding her brain. If she left now, what good would it do? She could find her way around, but physically, she no longer had the ability to run long distances. And what if the man who'd shot Nancy and Terry caught her? Or worse— what if he followed her? She'd lead him right to her innocent family.

He'd not hesitated to shoot Nancy. Or to take shots at her. There was no doubt in her mind that if she brought him to her *haus,* her *mamm*, Abigail, Rhoda and Betty would all be casualties. Her sweet *mamm* and sisters had suffered so much. Surely, *Gott* would not make them suffer more.

Unfortunately, her own faith had been shaken. Being innocent hadn't saved her father or Aaron, nor had it spared her mother, Caleb or herself from pain due to the injuries sustained. Since then, she doubted *Gott* would step in and protect them from harm.

It was up to her. She had to protect them.

Feeling like she couldn't breathe, Molly gulped for air. When she exhaled, another sob escaped. Suddenly, she couldn't stop the tears scalding her cheeks. She struggled to gain control of herself.

She felt, more than saw, Zeke move to her side and squat down beside her.

He didn't touch her, for which she was grateful. Any show of kindness would overwhelm her attempts to calm herself and regain her composure. Finally, she forced the tears to cease. Her ragged breathing was loud in the room, but at least she was no longer crying like a baby in front of him.

"Molly." His deep voice broke the stillness. "Molly, what happened? What do you mean, your mother and sisters are in danger? In danger from what?"

She shuddered. It took a moment to gather herself together to retell what had occurred. "I clean *hauser* to help pay the bills. On Tuesdays, I always clean for N-Nancy Stevens."

Another tear coursed down her cheek, and she stumbled on her client's name, but she continued the story. "This morning, there was no one home, but I had a key. I went in to clean, like I always do. I was almost done, when I heard shouting. Two men. I gathered my cleaning supplies and started to leave. I heard Nancy enter the *haus*. Then, she yelled. I heard—" She gulped, her stomach turning inside her. "I heard a gunshot."

Briefly, she noted his ashen complexion. What she'd said had been shocking, but she hadn't expected such an extreme reaction from him. Maybe he was extra sensitive since his own wife had died. Trauma affected people in different ways. She should probably stop talking.

Zeke wouldn't let her.

"What then, Molly?"

"I was wonderful scared. I put my boots on and tried to leave. But I was too noisy. The man who shot the gun, I think he shot Nancy, he ran out after me, still holding a gun. He shot at me. He would have killed me, but Terry ran out of the *haus* and tackled him. Terry yelled at me to go. I ran. Then I heard another gunshot. I think he shot Terry. He—the man with the gun—got into his car. He was searching for me."

Beside her, Zeke was still, like a statue carved in granite. She dropped her eyes and continued her story.

"I wanted to get help. But I had to hide. When I saw the van, I didn't even think of what trouble I could cause for you. I hid inside, knowing I needed to get away from there."

"The man who chased you, did he drive a dark yellow car?"

Her head jerked up. "*Ja!* Did you see him?"

He nodded. "He drove past the stable where I was working a few times. I haven't seen him here. I don't know that he'd have any way of knowing you were here. No one would figure you'd jump into an *Englisch* van."

Frowning, she tilted her head. She considered his words. It made sense that he wouldn't find her here. But what about her family? They didn't deserve any more pain. Of less importance, if she didn't contact them, they'd worry.

She lifted her chin. "If he discovers the name of the woman who cleaned the *haus*, he'd find my family. It wouldn't be difficult. I clean *haus* for several families in the area. I have to protect them. But how?"

He briefly touched her shoulder. "Molly, you're not alone. I will help you. We'll protect them."

He stood and paced away from her. Rubbing her palms against her eyes, she grimaced. They were gritty, like she'd fallen asleep in a pile of sand. Dropping her hands, she blinked, then tracked his figure as he walked back and forth across his workroom floor. It had been so long since she'd had anyone to lean on. Allowing someone to assist her now went against the grain.

But her family was at stake, and she couldn't do it alone. Zeke had been a friend in the past.

She didn't have a choice. If she wanted to do what was best for Terry and Nancy, as well as protect her *mamm* and younger sisters, she had to accept his help.

Hopefully, she wouldn't regret her decision.

He was in over his head again.

Zeke ran his hand over his short beard while he considered his options. The moment he'd promised his assistance, he'd regretted the impulsive words. His own wife had led a serial killer to their home, nearly killing Lissa, his older brother's wife, before the killer had turned on Iris and shot her. She'd died in Zeke's arms. He'd never seen the coldness in her before. Her actions had shocked him to the core, and still, he'd loved her. How had he been so blind?

Zeke knew himself well. He'd never been like his brothers, bold and forceful. He tended to sit back and observe before making observations. Likewise, he'd never been one to make rash decisions. His impulsive declaration had come out of nowhere. But he couldn't take it back. It was the right thing to do. She needed help.

But was he the right person for this task? Since Iris's betrayal and death, he'd begun second-guessing himself. He'd always prided himself on his astuteness, but he'd been so naive and trusting, it was embarrassing. It had cost him his wife, and the pain still left him breathless. He no longer trusted his own instincts.

More important, how could he promise to lend his aid to Molly? He wasn't exactly the best choice for a protector. Not if he couldn't even tell when the woman he'd loved had been deceiving him. Because she had been. She'd used him to help him achieve her goal.

His brother and Lissa had both counseled him to forgive Iris. After all, at the time, she'd been acting under duress. Traumatic situations sometimes caused people to act out of character. He understood that. On some level, he even agreed with it.

But he'd never seen the darkness in her, and she hadn't felt she could trust him with it. That was where the sting was. For whatever reason, she had felt she'd be better off leading Lissa to her probable death to save her brother rather than telling her husband that she feared her brother was in danger.

He'd failed her that much. In some ways, it seemed he owned a larger portion of the blame for her actions.

And now he was promising to help someone else. What if he failed her, too? He glanced back at Molly. Her eyes were following his every move, a question deep in her eyes. Sighing, he turned to face her.

"Are you sure you want to help me and the Stevens family? It's asking a lot of you." Her gaze zeroed in on his face, piercing him.

She voiced the questions without rancor. She didn't expect him to keep his word. Narrowing his gaze, he took in her defensive stance. Ah. It hit him then. She didn't like asking for help, but she was doing it anyway. Because she was terrified. Well, so was he. Terrified of failing again and seeing another woman, or anyone else, die in front of him. He met her eyes again. She was waiting for him to back off. He understood her doubts. It humbled him. What kind of coward ignored someone in need?

"*Ja.* I will help you." He cemented his commitment with five short words. Even now, he felt invisible chains pinning him down. He ignored the sensation. Zeke Bender had never broken a promise in his life. Once he gave his word, he stuck to it, even if it became difficult for him.

How he'd help her, he didn't know. First, he needed to get the whole picture.

"Molly, do you know what the man was doing at the *haus*? Had he broken in?"

Maybe she'd interrupted a robbery.

Her forehead creased and she delicately gnawed on her lower lip. Slowly, she shook her head. "*Nee.* I don't think so. The first time I heard the voices, they were raised, but Terry's voice didn't sound surprised. Not like someone had entered that he didn't know. Thinking back on it, his voice sounded defensive. You know? Like he'd been accused of something and was trying to make excuses."

Zeke understood. He had siblings. Gideon, honest as the day is long, had gotten himself into mischief frequently growing up. He'd tried to make excuses a few times before he learned he was better off telling the truth and admitting his mistakes.

"Did you hear any words that would tell you what kind of accusations?"

She shook her head. "*Nee.* The words were muffled by the closed door. I was uncomfortable and didn't want to be around to witness anything personal." Anguish spasmed across her face. Her shoulders slumped. "I was selfish. If I'd tried to listen instead of scrambling to escape without being seen, maybe I'd have been able to do something, ain't so?"

He hurried to interrupt this train of thought. "Absolutely not! If you had stayed, you would have been found and probably killed. Molly, what could you have done? You're Amish. You couldn't have used violence. And you already know he's more than willing to shoot one more person. He's tried to kill you already, *ja*? There's nothing you could have done there. Someone probably heard the shots and called the police. Even so, we can both get help."

She straightened her posture. "He would have killed me. *Ja.* I know you're right." Her words squeezed between her teeth. She was trying to convince herself and him.

He nodded. For a moment, they stared at each other. He swallowed. No new ideas came to mind. If Molly alone were in danger, he'd bring her to his parents' *haus*. But it was her whole family. He knew her brother was in a coma and her *daed* was dead, but she still had her *mamm* and several sisters to care for. He wasn't sure how many. When the districts had separated, there'd only been three children in the family. He knew from Caleb that there'd been more born into the family in the years that had followed.

Molly pushed herself to her feet and wandered aimlessly around his workshop. She picked up a hammer, then gently replaced it. She repeated the pattern with several other tools. After two or three minutes, she sank down into the wooden chair by his makeshift desk in the back of the room. Leaning her elbows on the arms of the chair, she rubbed her hands together briskly, as if she were warming them up, despite the fact that it was still nearly eighty degrees outside.

She looked so defeated. His heart ached, remembering that same look on his *mamm*'s face after his sister had disappeared twenty-four years earlier. His whole family had borne her loss, and the devastation her disappearance had wrought on them all. Even after she'd been returned to them two years ago, they couldn't be back to how they were. Isaiah hadn't returned. He hadn't heard from his older brother since he'd left twelve years earlier. And Micah was still *Englisch*, working as a deputy US marshal…

He stiffened. His brother worked in law enforcement. Just what they needed. He strode toward the desk and grabbed the portable phone off the charging base. It was for business only since the Amish didn't have personal phones. He hadn't had to use the number often, but he'd had the foresight to put his brother's contact information on speed dial.

"Are you calling the police?" She scrambled to her feet, wobbling slightly.

He shook his head. "I'm calling my brother Micah. He's a deputy US marshal."

THREE

Molly blinked, not sure she'd heard him correctly. She remembered Micah. He'd left the Amish community, she recalled. Still, the jump from Amish to deputy US marshal seemed a huge leap.

"A marshal?" she asked.

"*Ja*. Micah was obsessed with law enforcement after our sister disappeared. When he left, he joined the military, which he doesn't talk about, then the marshals when he returned to Ohio. He left before he was baptized, so we're still able to maintain a relationship with him."

"I'd forgotten about your sister."

Now she really felt bad. He'd had so much trauma in his life, and she was bringing more. What had his sister's name been? Catherine? Charity? *Nee*. Christina. That was it.

"Hey." He lowered the phone. She flicked her gaze up and met his warm eyes. "It's *gut. Ja*, someone abducted my sister many years ago. It had nothing to do with you. Also, my sister is back."

She gasped. "Christina is back! How?"

He nodded. "*Ja.* I will tell you about it later. But now, we have to concentrate on keeping you and your family safe, ain't so?"

Nodding, she rubbed her arms as he returned his attention to the phone in his hand.

Listening as he made the call, she again paced the confines of Zeke's workshop. Her body quivered with the desire to rush out and do something, anything. Which would be foolish. Zeke was correct. Calling the law was the next logical step. For the first time, she stopped to thank *Gott* for bringing her to Zeke when her world shattered with that gunshot earlier.

"*Ja*, I can do that."

She stopped pacing to see what Zeke could do. He pushed a button. "Micah, you're on speaker phone now."

"Molly?" a deep voice said in a calm, gentle tone. One that spoke of confidence and assured others to trust it.

"Ja?" She approached the phone.

"Molly, first of all, I need your address, and the address of the people you clean houses for."

She recited it from memory. Over the phone, she could hear a tapping sound. He was typing what she said into something. "Hold on a second. I have to relay this information."

When he began barking directions, she stared, amazed at the quick shift. Although she couldn't see him, she could tell he'd taken the phone away from his mouth. Who was he talking to? She didn't hear any other people around.

"He's probably on another phone, or on a radio," Zeke whispered.

"I can't believe that's the same man I was just talking to."

Zeke chuckled softly beside her. "It's impressive, isn't it?"

Impressive hadn't been the word in her mind. Maybe intimidating. Possibly scary. Probably not impressive.

"I'll be there soon," Micah said, then disconnected abruptly.

Thirty minutes later, Molly couldn't stop

looking back and forth between Zeke and his older brother, US Deputy Marshal Micah Bender. Except for Zeke's beard and Micah's uniform, they could almost have been twins. She didn't remember them looking so alike when they were younger, when the years separating them made a bigger difference.

Micah didn't come alone, either. He brought with him a man he introduced as Sergeant Steve Beck.

"Steve! Glad you came with him." Zeke greeted the policeman.

He was? She stared at Zeke, completely baffled by his attitude. Sure, they needed the police right now. Typically, however, the Amish tended to avoid involving the *Englisch* law in anything except the most serious of issues. He greeted Sergeant Beck as a trusted friend, not an outsider.

She felt someone watching her and swung her head around to find herself under observation. Micah nodded at her. In response, she raised an eyebrow. His stare was direct and penetrating. It unnerved her. The Amish didn't stare like that. It was considered rude. But Micah wasn't Amish anymore, she reminded herself. Maybe that was why he didn't know better.

"Molly, I remember your family. I was sorry to learn about what happened to them and to your fiancé."

Zeke's head nodded in agreement. She should have known he'd be aware of the accident. She hadn't mentioned it to him, or said anything about Aaron, because what had happened last year had no bearing on the horrible events earlier in the day. Although, had her father and Aaron still been alive, she would have turned to them, and not bothered a former acquaintance with her trials.

"Denke."

Micah's phone rang. He excused himself and went to answer it.

Zeke made his way to her side. "Are you *gut*?"

She shrugged. "Not really. It's all I can do to keep standing." She nodded slightly toward Micah. "I don't remember him being that intense when I knew your family."

He hesitated. "You don't remember the details about what happened to our sister, do you?"

Her head turned so she could meet his eyes.

She remembered growing up with Micah, Isaiah, Zeke and Gideon. "Not the specifics. I remember hearing *Mamm* and *Daed* talking about it over the years. They said your sister had disappeared. She was only two or three."

He nodded. "*Ja.* She was two. Micah never forgave himself. That changed him and directed most of his decisions."

She felt terrible. She opened her mouth to apologize.

"It's all *gut*," he assured her. "We have my sister back."

The police officer, Sergeant Beck, stepped closer to them. "She's married to me."

Now she was really baffled. "An Amish woman married to an *Englischer*?"

Micah hung up the phone and approached.

"We'll tell you about her later," Zeke murmured.

Later? She didn't think there would be a later. She wanted to go home and make sure her family was safe.

Static crackled through the room. A series of electronic whistles burst from a small device attached to the shoulder of the police officer married to Zeke's sister. A female voice issued from the device, spitting out a stream of jargon. She understood the Stevenses' address, but nothing else.

"What?" She nodded at the device. "What's going on?"

The voice continued, but she didn't understand all the technical terms.

"I called for the police and emergency services to go to the house where the shooting happened before I arrived. The police arrived. The ambulance took a little longer to get there."

Molly perked up. "Ambulance? They're alive."

She read the denial in his gaze.

The radio burst to life again. This time, she clearly heard the word *coroner*.

"Coroner? Someone's dead." Numbness rolled through her mind and took over her nervous system.

Zeke appeared at her side. He slid an arm around her shoulders. Not a gesture of romance or flirtation. He was holding her upright. "Molly."

"Who is dead? Micah? Zeke? Who?"

Micah took a step toward her. "Nancy didn't survive, Molly. I'm so sorry."

Molly's whole body spasmed with the news, but she didn't fall. "And Terry?"

"He's alive. They don't know yet if he'll make it. His father, Frank, is being told as we speak. Someone will make sure he gets to the hospital."

"Poor Frank. And Nancy. She was so kind to me."

"Molly? One more thing. I've sent my partner over to your house to keep watch over your family."

She sat down on the desk chair. Her family would be safe. They would be protected. "Do they know who did this? Or why?"

"I don't have that information yet. I will let you know when I do. Right now, I need you to tell me everything that happened, Molly. You might be our only hope of catching him."

She squeezed her hands into fists. She needed to go home. "But I've told Zeke everything. And you already sent help."

He held up a hand to halt her complaints. "I understand. But the more we know, the less time we'll waste trying to figure out what happened. Plus, it will be safer for everyone if we know what we're dealing with."

All three men wore resolute expressions,

although Zeke's was tempered with compassion. And wariness. If she were him, she'd probably want nothing to do with this nasty situation.

The only way to get back to her family was to give them what they wanted. "I clean for Nancy every Tuesday. Since my *daed* died, my sister Abigail and I have worked to bring in the money to pay the bills."

She told them how she'd been cleaning and heard the shouts.

"Did you recognize the voices?" Sergeant Beck asked.

She shook her head. "Not the one voice. I recognized Terry's voice."

"What about what they said?" Micah took over the questioning.

"*Nee.* I didn't understand any of it." She clasped her hands in her lap to keep them from trembling. Her stomach ached. It was hard to sit straight in the chair. She continued the story. Despite her best efforts, several tears escaped when she told how Nancy had screamed before the shot rang out.

When she finished the story, the three men were silent for so long, it made her itch to yell at them to say something.

"Can I go home now?" she finally demanded.

Surprisingly, Zeke was the one who responded. "Molly, I don't think that's a wonderful *gut* idea."

She scowled at him. "Why not? The police have been notified. Someone is at my *haus* right now."

"*Ja*, right now. But they can't stay there," Micah said, leaning against the desk and folding his arms loosely across his torso. "Even if they could, we don't know who the shooter is or why he was there. You saw his face, so he saw yours."

She shook her head. "At least let me go back and explain what happened. I'll be safe while the police are there."

Micah opened his mouth. She saw Zeke motion to him. "Fine. But you're not going alone. I'm going to go with you."

Why had he said that? Zeke wanted to take the words back, but it was too late. Guilt pierced him at the relief dawning on her countenance. He had no reason to go with her. His brother and brother-in-law were both *Englisch* law. Although he didn't hold with it, Micah and Steve were armed with guns and phones. If something went wrong, they would be able to step in and render assistance.

Unbidden, the image of Micah grabbing a gun to search for Lissa at his *haus* came to mind. They'd not found Lissa, but had found Iris, bleeding out. So much death and violence. His own convictions to never pick up a weapon and use it against another person solidified in his mind. He would never kill.

He would, however, willingly step in front of a bullet to save another.

Micah gave him a look that was just shy of a glare. He furrowed his brow. Ah. He'd inserted himself into the investigation. He'd seen that look before. *Ja*, his overprotective older brother was planning on protecting him again. Micah tended to take his responsibility too far. This time, however, Zeke was not his responsibility.

He returned the look with interest. He'd promised Molly he would help her, and he meant to follow through.

Molly closed the distance between them in two steps, her elbow nudging his side as she placed herself at his side. He could have moved away from her. Should have. Except he was strangely hesitant.

Micah let the issue rest. They all moved out to his SUV. Micah and Steve got into the front seat, leaving Molly and Zeke in the back. For once in his life, Zeke wished he were more outgoing. Molly was as tense as a mouse being hunted by a cat, but he couldn't think of any words to soothe her. The foot between them seemed an unbridgeable chasm. He couldn't even breach the distance by reaching across and taking her hand to comfort her because she had her arms crossed, her hands buried under her biceps. Molly had closed herself off.

So, they rode together in silence. He remembered the Schultz place, even though it had been years since he'd been there. The unmarked police cruiser in the driveway seemed out of place next to the unhitched buggy.

"Abigail forgot to put the buggy in the barn again." The commonplace words seemed starkly out of place considering the menace surrounding her situation. Molly pressed her face close to the window, angling her head to peer all around.

She was searching for danger. Or for the

face of a killer. He stiffened in response, ready to pull her back at the first sign of imminent peril. When she sighed and relaxed, he knew she'd seen nothing alarming and followed suit.

Once Micah parked the car, she started to reach for the handle. Zeke touched her hand. Her head whipped around, her face startled. "Wait. They'll tell us when it's safe."

She withdrew her hand from his but didn't make another move for the door. His skin heated at her silent rebuff. He hadn't planned on touching her. It had been an instinctive move.

He never let instinct rule his actions. Every move he made was deliberate.

Or so it had been.

Irritated, his foot tapped the floorboard while they waited for Micah and Steve to let them out. *Ach.* They were taking too long. The whole situation was wonderful trying and becoming more so by the minute.

A knock on the window startled him. Next to him, Molly jerked at the sound, too. Glancing out, he encountered Steve's amused grin. He kept his face blank and opened the door. Molly did the same on the other side of the

SUV. He met her in front of the vehicle. Her gaze wouldn't settle on one place or object.

"Molly?" Merely watching her made him ready to jump out of his skin.

"I feel like I'm being watched," she whispered. He looked over his shoulder. Steve hadn't heard her.

"Where?"

She shrugged. "Am I imagining it?"

He saw her shiver. Unease built inside him. "We need to get inside the *haus*."

If someone was watching, they were standing out in the open. Carefully, trying not to be obvious, he rearranged his position so he was at her shoulder, slightly behind her back. If someone tried to shoot at her, he would plant himself in the path of the bullet. He might not be able to wield a weapon, but that didn't mean he couldn't intercept one used against others.

An officer was waiting for them at the porch. He wasn't wearing a police uniform. His badge looked the same as Micah's. The deputy US marshal had said his partner was watching over her family.

"Anything interesting, Parker?" Micah asked, his voice casual.

The man he'd called Parker shook his head. "Not yet, but I'm not letting down my guard."

Micah nodded. "Molly, Zeke. This is my partner, Deputy US Marshal Parker Gates. You can call him Marshal, or Parker."

"Thank you for watching out for my family, Parker," she told him, an uneasy expression stamped on her pretty features. Zeke imagined calling him by his first name felt normal and odd at the same time. Normal because in the Amish community, most people were called by their first names and not by titles. Odd, though, because Parker Gates was not Amish. His profession and way of life were far outside anything in her experience.

"It's my pleasure, Miss Schultz. Why don't you all get inside where it's safe? I'll keep watch out here."

Micah opened the door for them and moved aside so Molly and Zeke could enter the *haus*. Steve and Micah both stood and took one long look around before crossing the threshold and closing the door behind them. Zeke kept himself between Molly and the door until it was securely locked.

Zeke sighed, then smiled when she echoed the sound. It was a relief to enter the *haus*.

Although no one said anything, he felt the tension in the air ease once the front door was secured.

Abigail already had the evening meal ready for them. Molly's *mamm* insisted the officers join them. Molly pushed her mother's wheelchair to the head of the table and called to the other sisters. The small group sat around the table to partake of the delicious food. A bowl of salad with homemade dressing was passed around first. It was followed by chicken and homemade noodles, mashed potatoes and gravy, and homemade bread with apple butter. Zeke tried to eat. Normally, he had a healthy appetite. Not tonight. The food sat like lead in his stomach. He wasn't the only one struggling to eat. At his side, Molly pushed the food around on her plate. Energy seemed to zip from her, zinging in the air. The younger girls were the only two at the table who ate as if nothing were out of the ordinary. They hadn't been born when the district had split.

"Rhoda is thirteen," Molly murmured, "And Elizabeth is nine. We call her Betty."

She must have seen him glancing at them. He nodded his thanks.

Zeke twisted on the bench and watched the pain wash up Molly's face, now pale with exhaustion and anguish. Her gaze remained locked on the plate in front of her. If she had lifted her gaze, he expected the tears would be seconds away from spilling.

Something thudded against the *haus*. A hush fell over the entire room. Even nine-year-old Betty's head whipped up, her mouth hanging wide open.

Steve rose silently from the table, motioning for the rest of them to remain seated. He edged his way to the window. Micah was already at the back door. The two men silently peered out, searching for the danger. Micah slipped out to continue the hunt. Zeke muttered a prayer for his safety under his breath. It felt rusty. His prayer life had lost its zest after Iris had died. But he wouldn't watch his brother face danger and not cover him with prayer.

A moment later, Micah pounded on the entrance, announcing himself.

Zeke rushed over, Molly on his heels. He looked out and saw Micah holding the body of the officer who'd been guarding the *haus*. With an exclamation, he threw the door wide open, then helped Micah bring the man inside, vaguely aware that Molly was ordering the *kinder* to go into the other room.

Blood was spreading over the man's shirt, creeping like a deadly army outward. But he was breathing.

"Call 911," Micah barked.

Steve already had his phone out.

Molly. Where was Molly?

Spinning around, Zeke spotted her standing with her back to the open door, her hands covering her mouth. Behind her, a shadow moved. He didn't even think. Diving toward her, he knocked her out of the doorway. They rolled onto the floor.

A knife whizzed into the room, making a solid thunk as it hit the wall, the blade sinking into the wood, vibrating with the force of impact.

Had he not pushed her out of its path, it would have sunk deep into Molly's back.

Whoever had been searching for her knew where she lived.

FOUR

Zeke bounced back off the floor and kicked the door shut so hard, the walls shuddered. A quick glance around the room showed everyone else was safe. Shocked, the kinder were crying, but they were not harmed. He turned back to the woman on the floor next to him.

"Molly, are you all right?"

She sat up, grimacing, but nodding her head. *"Ja.* Check on your brother."

He crossed the room in two steps and knelt at his brother's side. Parker, his brother's partner, was pale but alert. The bloody stain continued to grow.

"Grab me a dish towel," Micah growled.

Zeke leaped up and grabbed a clean towel from the drawer he'd seen Molly pull one out of earlier. Was it only thirty minutes ago?

Dropping down beside his brother again, he handed him the cloth.

"Micah, I need to go after this guy," Steve said. "Can you stay on the line with 911?"

"Zeke," Micah commanded, "I need you to press down on this wound. Keep the pressure on it."

Zeke leaned forward and pushed firmly on the folded towel. Parker groaned, but other than that, didn't complain. Micah grabbed the phone from Steve. The officer cracked the door open and peered outside, his narrowed eyes scanning the area. After a few breathless seconds, he pulled the door open wider and slipped through it. When it closed behind him, a thick silence descended, broken only by Parker's harsh breathing.

Micah held the phone to his ear and began barking orders.

"This is Deputy Marshal Micah Bender. Sergeant Steve Beck is going after the unsub. How long until backup and the ambulance arrive?"

"The ambulance is still ten minutes out, Marshal. Backup is on the way. They should arrive in under five minutes."

Zeke's mind whirled. Ten minutes. Did

Parker have ten minutes? He glanced down at the injured deputy marshal. The dishcloth felt damp, wadded up in his hand and pressed against the wound. It was stained red where the blood had seeped through. His glance collided with Parker's. He had no idea what condition the other man was in. Zeke hadn't been trained in first aid.

"Parker," Micah rumbled beside them. "How are you holding up?"

"I'll be fine," the injured man rasped. "He surprised me. Whoever he is, he knows how to use knives."

"What can I do?" Molly appeared at his side.

He didn't want her standing in the middle of the room. "Get down. We don't know where he is."

He being the man running amok throwing knives like they were toys. This kind of violence, even after his wife had been murdered, continued to shock him. He never understood how someone could willfully hurt another. But that didn't mean he wouldn't be on his guard to protect Molly and her family. "Keep your family away from the windows and doors. The ambulance will be here soon."

He didn't want them in the area when that door opened. He also didn't want to leave them unprotected. He was crouched between where his brother knelt next to Parker on the floor and where Molly stood grouped together with her sisters and her mother. That way, if his brother decided he needed his help, Zeke could be there in an instant. In the same vein, if an assailant burst through the door, Zeke could shield the women from harm.

A sudden shout outside disrupted his musing.

Micah stood and dashed to the window. He peered out, his head swiveling back and forth as he looked in all directions.

He had to be frustrated. Micah was a man of action. But he couldn't leave the house, not with civilians inside who needed his protection, or with his partner down. Until the cops got there, that left Steve on his own to handle whatever was happening outside.

Zeke's hand tightened at his side. He ground his teeth together to keep from saying what was on his mind. He liked his brother-in-law a lot. Steve had been very good to Joss, and the family was very grateful that he'd brought their lost girl back to them. It was sometimes hard to think of her as Joss. All his life, his lost sister had been called Christina. The name didn't matter, though. She was back.

He needed to be prepared for the worst. But first, he had another responsibility.

"Molly. Is there a room with no outside entrance? No outside doors or windows?"

If he could remove Molly and her family from this room, they would no longer be a distraction. It would be impossible to concentrate his efforts on helping his brother if he was constantly keeping vigil over the lovely young woman and her family.

He frowned. Now was not the time to notice such things. It was literally a life-or-death situation. "Just for a little while until Steve gets back."

Startled, Molly stared at Zeke, noting how his harsh tone conflicted with the compassion and concern in his eyes. Nothing in her young life had taught her to expect deliberate violence. Even the accident, which had killed her father and her fiancé, even that had been a result of foolish recklessness and not any malicious design.

This situation was completely out of her experience.

"*Ja.* There is a small pantry that would work."

"Go there and wait."

At the window, Micah nodded his approval of the plan.

Molly herded her three siblings and her mother back to the small, enclosed pantry. She left the door cracked open so a stream of the light from the kitchen windows filtered through. It had to be close to seven thirty in the evening. Fortunately, in July, the sun wouldn't set for over an hour, so the narrow room lined with shelves filled with canned goods and bags of flour, sugar and rice had enough light for her to make out shapes, although she couldn't see her family's faces. Betty whimpered.

"Shh. It's all right, Betty. We're all here together."

She hoped she wasn't lying to her youngest sister. A few hours ago, she wouldn't have doubted their safety with the overwhelming police presence in the *haus*. That was before two people were gunned down in the space of ten minutes and a madman waving a gun had chased her through suburban Ohio. Or before a deputy US marshal had been stabbed right outside her home.

Now, she didn't know what it would take for her to feel safe again.

Once more, her mind glossed over the idea of praying, but she hardened her heart against the idea. *Gott* had already shown He didn't care, hadn't He?

It was up to her. And possibly Zeke.

She had to admit, she was seeing a different side to him than she had when they were *kinder*. She'd noticed how he had deliberately placed his own body in front of her family. And she had been impressed in spite of herself.

"It's so quiet," Abigail murmured, her voice low.

Molly nodded. Then wondered if they could see the motion. "*Ja*, it is. I hope that's a good sign."

Wouldn't there be shouting, or banging, or something if it wasn't all right?

"Molly, I'm scared."

Betty stood against the opposite side, her head barely clearing the second shelf. Sliding her feet rather than picking them up to

avoid tripping over any items on the floor,
Molly moved beside her baby sister and gently placed her arms around the girl, giving
her a light squeeze. She wouldn't tell her she
wasn't scared. Because she was. They were,
all of them, in mortal peril.

"I know, Betty. I know. I'm here. Zeke will
tell us when we can come out."

Her sister's quiet sniff broke her heart. Taking in a deep breath to calm herself, she inhaled a swirl of dust in the air. She turned her
head to cough lightly.

"Why do we have to stay here? Why can't
we stay in the kitchen?"

"*Ach* my *kind*, this is where we are safe."
Mamm's soft voice intruded.

"But…"

"Hush, Betty." Molly kissed the top of her
head. "There are no windows here, so no one
can see us, *ja*? And no one can enter and surprise us."

"How did that policeman get hurt?"

Molly's mind went blank. She didn't know
how to answer that one.

"Someone stabbed him," Rhoda announced
in a loud, harsh whisper. "Don't you know
anything?"

"Quiet, Rhoda." Her *mamm*'s gentle voice interrupted the argument before it could completely erupt. "Don't be unkind to your sister."

Molly bit her lip. She would have given her sister a sterner scold, but they were not her *kinder*. She held back the harsh words on the tip of her tongue out of love and respect for her mother.

The girls continued to whisper. Although they were softer, her pulse pounded in her ears. If someone entered the hall outside the pantry, she wouldn't hear them because of the activity in the small storage area.

She blew out a hard breath and forced herself to remain calm. "We need to all stop making noise so I can hear what's happening outside."

With a few grumbles and the sound of bodies shifting where they were crouched around her mother's wheelchair, they settled down. She only heard breathing and the occasional sniffle from Betty. The dark made it difficult to tell if her sister was sniffing because of her allergies or if she was crying. Probably the first one. Betty had never been overly emotional. She tended to take things in stride. Rhoda, on the other hand, lived for drama.

Cramps seized Molly's leg. She clenched her teeth around an exclamation of pain. She had no choice; she needed to bear it for a few minutes more. Zeke told them to go to this room, so if their attacker somehow entered the *haus*, he wouldn't see them. Nor would he be able to see her or the others from an outside window. Had they been in the kitchen still, anyone could have looked in and seen them. Like every Amish *haus* in the district, none of the windows had curtains.

A few more minutes passed. She heard footsteps moving toward the pantry. One of her sisters gasped. It sounded like Rhoda. She didn't blame her. The suspense was too much. She braced herself against the shelves and carefully stood. The door opened and light flooded in.

Zeke stood in the entrance.

"*Cumme.* Steve has returned." His calm voice was like an anchor.

The Schultz family filed out of the pantry in a haphazard manner. Molly brought up the rear, behind her mother's wheelchair. Steve stood near Parker, keeping an eye on the door. She couldn't help but notice his disgruntled expression. Her stomach bottomed out. He wasn't happy. Obviously, his mission hadn't gone as planned.

Micah returned to the room. He glanced around, his gaze touching them all.

"What did you find?" she asked softly, her gaze traveling between Micah and Steve.

Steve responded without removing his glance from the door. "He had someone waiting by in a car. I'm sorry. He got away before I could get near him."

Molly shivered. Whoever had chased her, the person responsible for Nancy's and possibly Terry's deaths, and the person who had stabbed a deputy marshal, was out there, running free. And he knew where she lived and what she looked like.

FIVE

They got away.

Zeke stood outside the front door with his brother and brother-in-law watching the backup law enforcement officers combing the area around the *haus*. He mulled the implications in his mind, striving to understand how such a thing happened. With all the modern advances at their fingertips, all the knowledge, the weapons and the high-tech gadgets available to *Englisch* law enforcement, a potential killer had still managed to escape. He couldn't wrap his mind around it. It solidified for him the fact that *Gott* was the only reliable power in the universe. Only He could work all things out and truly keep Molly and her family safe.

Micah muttered darkly beside him.

"What?"

His brother shook his head. "It's not Steve's fault. Sometimes the suspect escapes. It is frustrating, though. We were so close."

Nodding his understanding, Zeke pivoted slightly until Molly came into his line of sight. She caught his eye and smiled, a tight, forced expression. What an amazing woman. She'd been shot at, nearly speared with a knife and forced to hide in a pantry while an armed man ran amok outside her *haus*. She didn't complain, or stomp around letting the world know she was upset. And she was. If her shoulders tensed any more, they'd snap. But still, she smiled and busied herself caring for her family and keeping watch over the injured deputy marshal who'd been bleeding on her kitchen floor. Amazing.

"Your friend is impressing me," Micah said, echoing his own thoughts.

"*Ja.* She is impressing me, too. Do you remember her family well?" He took his eyes off her briefly to look at his brother.

Micah shrugged. "Some. I remember Caleb, and her parents, mostly. I don't recall much about Molly."

Edging closer to Micah, he kept his voice low so the others wouldn't hear him. "So, what do we do now? Obviously, they can't stay here. Molly isn't safe, and neither is her family, until this man is caught."

Micah rubbed his hand over his mouth. Zeke recognized the gesture. It meant Micah was mentally gathering all the pieces together.

"More than that. We are looking for more than one person."

"I agree." Steve stepped into the light. "For him to get away that quick, he had to have an accomplice."

An accomplice. His gut twisted. He held his breath, waiting for his rolling stomach to settle before he spoke. "Someone is helping him."

Both officers dipped their chins once in acknowledgment.

"It's a bit scary, you know, realizing how much evil exits in our peaceful town." Discouraged, he left them and entered the *haus*. He strode to Molly without thinking.

"What's happening out there?" She jerked her head in the direction of Micah and Steve.

"Nothing *gut*. Steve and Micah are discussing the man who threw a knife at you. They think he had help."

She frowned but didn't seem shocked. "I actually wondered about that."

"Why?" Steve asked.

They both startled.

"I didn't hear you *cumme* in," Zeke remarked.

"Sorry." Steve turned his gaze back to Molly.

She squirmed under the attention, a light rosy flush swirling into her face. But she met their eyes with a level stare of her own. "I didn't see much when I was standing in the doorway. But something about the way the person stood, I don't think it was the same man who shot at me."

"Are you sure?" Micah entered the conversation, shutting the door behind him.

"*Nee.* But that's the impression I got."

"I'm inclined to agree with her," Steve said. "I don't know why the perp would change methods. A gun for the first attack and then a knife here."

"So you wouldn't hear him."

They all spun to stare at Zeke so fast, he took a step back. It was intense. "It makes sense to me. If he wanted to get to Molly, Parker was in the way. If he'd shot him—"

"Any advantage he had would vanish," Micah finished his statement. "It's a good theory. I hope it's true."

He understood. If it was the same person, that would mean they had fewer people coming after Molly and her family. "I'm still a little worried about what happens next. I hate to say it again, but I don't think this is a safe place for your family anymore, Molly."

Steve glanced over his shoulder at Parker. The deputy marshal had slipped into sleep. The bleeding had stopped, and he seemed stable. At least he hoped he was. Keeping an eye on him for a few seconds, Zeke was relieved to see his chest rising and falling as he breathed in and out. He was alive. That was the one positive amid all of this. They were all alive. Thus far, the attacks had failed. Hopefully that would remain true.

"I agree. But we can't do anything until the ambulance comes."

Micah had barely spat the last word out of his mouth when the ambulance pulled into the driveway, its wide wheels rolling along the edges, crushing the first inch of grass on either side. It halted with a soft, fast squeal right in front of the door.

Zeke tapped Molly on the shoulder. He waited until he had her attention before speaking. "We should go farther into the *haus*, ain't so? Let the ambulance crew take care of Parker without giving Micah and Steve cause to worry about us."

She nodded and hurried to urge her sisters into the next room. Zeke moved behind her mother's wheelchair and gently pushed it behind them.

"*Denke*, Zeke." The woman smiled at him over her shoulder. He blinked, distracted by Esther Schultz's lovely smile. She had passed that smile on to her oldest daughter. Despite the grim circumstances, it tugged an answering smile from him.

As a medical team came into the *haus* and tended to Parker, Zeke tucked the wheelchair between the chairs occupied by Rhoda and Betty, then crossed the room to join Molly and Abigail along the wall. The family avoided standing near the windows, he noted. From the wall, the angle allowed them to view the paramedics when they loaded Parker into the ambulance. One of them climbed in back after him. The other stood and spoke with Micah for a minute before she shut the door and hopped into the driver's seat.

Abigail left them to join her mother.

"The sun's going down," Molly whispered, a wistful tinge layered into her sooth-ing voice.

Soon it would be dark. Zeke hated to think about these women in this *haus* alone at night. If they hadn't been safe with two deputy mar-shals and a police sergeant inside, plus two additional officers outside, he had zero con-fidence that they would be safe once the sun went down. He couldn't say that, though. Rhoda and Betty might be listening to this conversation.

Instead, he made a noncommittal noise and settled himself against the white wall close enough that he could reach out and hold her hand if he wanted to. Of course, he didn't want to. What had gotten into him to even think that? A young woman like Molly wouldn't have any interest in a cynical widower like himself. Especially not one with his history of failures. She needed someone youthful, like herself, and filled with optimism.

She deserved that.

"We can't stay here," she continued. "Not after all that's happened. If he attacked us in daylight, what would keep him from killing us in our sleep?"

Zeke tightened his body to ward off the

shudder he felt twitching his shoulder blades. She wasn't wrong. Danger stalked her family. Hopefully, Steve and Micah had a plan.

Once she was safe, he could return home to his life, secure in the knowledge that he had done his part. That's what he wanted. He hadn't meant to become this involved.

Whether he'd meant to become involved or not, the thought of resuming his life where he'd left it held no joy for him. In less than six hours, Molly Schultz and her family had cracked the peaceful monotony of his world.

But what would become of her?

Molly fought back the rising panic, blocking her throat and making breathing difficult. She couldn't snatch her gaze from the ambulance turning around in the driveway. The vehicle drove off, creating a sick feeling in her belly. Surely, they wouldn't be left here?

Suddenly the *haus* she'd grown up in, the refuge she'd relied on her entire life, felt like a giant trap. The illusion of security had been ripped aside, the way one ripped off a Band-Aid. Quick, with no warning. Had it only been this morning since she'd waved at Adele's *kinder* in their buggy, wishing for some of her own?

That desire, the one that had haunted her since the accident, took a back seat to the new desire, the drive to protect the family she had left. She couldn't do that here.

Not anymore.

"Molly, it will be fine." Zeke's soft voice was inches from her right ear.

Her head jerked up and around until she found herself staring into Zeke Bender's bright blue eyes. How had she not seen how warm they were? Those eyes promised her she'd be cared for.

She shook off the ridiculous thoughts. Soon he'd be gone. She was all her family had to rely on. They came first. Any thoughts or inclinations she'd ever had that her life would include romance had died with Aaron. Now was not the time to develop a crush on a man out of her reach.

Micah and Steve entered the room, their faces almost twin masks of efficiency and confidence.

"The ambulance left with Parker," Micah stated. "The backup from the police department is still searching the perimeter."

Molly started and glanced toward the window. She'd been so caught up in her own thoughts, she'd never seen the police car arrive. Two officers roamed the yard, flashlights sweeping before them.

"What are they looking for? I thought the man you were searching for was gone?" She frowned, confused.

Steve's head bobbed twice in a nod. "That's correct. They're looking for any evidence he or they might have left behind."

"Molly can't stay here, Steve," Zeke announced, his tone brisk.

Zeke's voice shocked her. She hadn't thought he could speak so forcefully.

Steve held out his hands. "I know, I know. Trust me, Zeke. We're not abandoning the family. In fact, I suggest they go and pack an overnight bag. We'll need to head into the police station first, but then we'll figure out where they can stay tonight. They'll probably be in a hotel with some security."

"A hotel?" *Mamm* spoke up, her voice quivering. "Oh, I don't know. I don't want to leave our home."

She also didn't want to get too involved with the *Englisch* law. Molly bit back a sigh.

"*Mamm*, we need to let the police and the marshals do their job. This man killed someone today. Maybe two people." She hoped Terry remained alive. "They're trying to kill me. I can't risk the girls or you."

"*Gott* will provide," Esther announced.

He hadn't provided thirteen months ago. Molly pressed her lips together to keep the bitter words in. It wouldn't help. Her mother didn't know how broken her faith was. It wasn't something she talked about.

Zeke pushed himself off the wall and swiftly crossed to Esther's side, kneeling down beside the wheelchair so he could meet her eyes without her needing to crane her neck back. "I understand. But it won't be forever. It would protect your *kinder*."

When Esther smiled and gave in without any further argument, Molly almost fell over. My, he had a way abour him. She'd been so sure her mother would be nearly impossible to convince. She didn't question it, though, not wanting to give her mother time to change her mind.

Herding her sisters back to their rooms, she packed her own bag and then gathered what her mother would need before returning to her two youngest sisters and monitoring their progress. From their whispers and giggles while they packed, she gathered the unique opportunity to ride in a police car was a huge motivator. Abigail joined them, her bag gripped in one hand, and listened to the giggles for a few seconds before rolling her eyes at Molly.

"Are they almost done?"

"We're done," Rhoda replied.

Molly and Abigail both took a bag and inspected it, making sure the girls hadn't forgotten anything in their haste.

When their satchels were packed to her satisfaction, she led the small group to the kitchen. Zeke, Steve and Micah loaded the suitcases into the police cars.

"Do you want me to drop you off at your place, Zeke?" Micah questioned his brother.

Molly reacted without thinking and grabbed on to Zeke's arm.

He patted her hand. "Not yet. I'll go to the station with them. Just in case."

In case of what she didn't know. He wasn't a cop, or a marshal. He had no authority at all. And if they were attacked, Zeke was a pacifist, the same as any other Amish man. He wouldn't pick up a weapon to defend them.

All the same, the constriction in her chest eased, knowing he'd be there. It was foolish. But she didn't care. Esther and her three younger daughters joined Micah and Steve in the SUV. Molly and Zeke were led to the cruiser with the two new officers.

Looking around, she began to chuckle.

"What's so funny?"

"I feel like we've been arrested. I never realized there'd be a divider between us and them." She pointed to the barrier between the front and back seats.

He grinned back at her. "It does feel that way."

Once they arrived at the precinct, all lightheartedness died suddenly. The reality of their situation descended like a black cloud. Surrounded by officers, the family and Zeke were hurried into the single-story brick building. Within moments, they were locked inside the conference room with the officers and Chief Spencer, Steve Beck's boss.

"Bring me up to speed, Sergeant," Chief Spencer requested in his deep, slow voice.

Molly hung back while Steve straightened

and became every inch a focused police sergeant. He recounted the day's events without embellishment. Somehow, that made the horror so much more profound.

A warm hand gripped hers. Zeke. She latched onto the comfort he offered and held tight. She squeezed his hand so hard, her fingers tingled after a few moments. Still, she couldn't let go. All the agony, all the fear she'd felt all day pressed down on her, crushing her under its weight. In that moment, she didn't know how she would get through the next few minutes, let alone the next few hours, without Zeke by her side.

The chief listened without interrupting. When they fell silent, he asked a few clarifying questions.

"Miss Schultz." The chief approached her. *"Ja?"*

"I understand you saw the man who shot Nancy Stevens this afternoon?"

"I did."

"Do you think you'd recognize him if you saw his picture?" His kind gaze lingered on her face.

She shivered as the man's image filled

her mind. "*Ja.* I don't think I will ever forget him."

"I'm sorry you've been through this. I also apologize because I need you to help us catch him."

Tilting her head, she considered him. "You need my help? What can I do?"

He smiled. "Indeed. You are the one person who can help us identify him. We have a database with pictures of criminals who have records. If you could go over it, maybe we can find his identity. That would let us send out word to other departments. We could widen the net, and have more people searching for him."

She wanted to help. If she was ever going to have any sense of peace, she needed to know that he was not wandering the streets anymore. However, she'd never even touched a computer screen. Oh, she knew some Amish teenagers used computers or tablets while they were on *rumspringa*. She never had any interest in that kind of technology.

Since she was a full member of the Amish community, there was no reason for her to use that technology. She didn't need it in her business. It wasn't allowed in their homes.

The question was, was she allowed to use it while helping the police?

"I would like to help," she responded slowly. "I think it would be allowed. I'd feel more comfortable about it if my bishop gave his approval."

The chief nodded, corners of his mouth turning down slightly. Not exactly in a frown. "I can send some officers to his home. Is it Bishop Hershberger?"

She blinked, surprised. "*Ja*. I didn't realize you knew him."

"We've worked with him before. I've found him to be accommodating in the past. In the meantime, I do have some picture files you can look at. They're older, but maybe it will be enough."

Betty let out a loud, exaggerated yawn. Chief Spencer chuckled. "Maybe we can send your family to the hotel and you can join them later. Unless you're too tired tonight?"

Although he said the words, she sensed his eagerness to start searching for the shooter. And she couldn't blame him. She, too, was anxious.

"I'd rather start looking at the pictures tonight, if you don't mind."

Relief bloomed on his face. "Not at all! I'll have them set out for you."

Two officers whisked her family out of the conference room. She watched them leave, torn. While she knew she'd be joining them soon, her heart ached at the separation, knowing danger followed them all.

Soon, a female officer entered the room. "Miss Schultz, I'm Lieutenant Kathy Bartlett. If you'll come with me, you can begin looking at images."

Molly agreed and followed, aware of Zeke close behind her. They moved to a smaller room. Several photo albums, about four inches thick, waited for them on the sturdy rectangular table. A pitcher of water and two empty glasses sat on a tray near the end of the table.

"Help yourselves to water. Take your time. There's no pressure here. We might not have his photo, so if you don't find a match, don't worry."

Zeke poured both of them a glass of water while she sat and began paging through the first album. He handed her a glass. Her fingers brushed his as they closed around the icy glass. The shiver that ran through her had nothing to do with the cold dish or the condensation beading on the exterior. He backed away, the tips of his ears and his cheeks glowing with sudden warmth. She ducked her head, knowing her face was in the same condition.

They didn't speak for the next hour. She closed one album and reached for the second one. The door burst open. Lieutenant Bartlett rushed in.

"Change of plans." Her rapid movement and strident voice made Molly's heart pound. Something had happened. "I got news that the car carrying your family was fired on."

Both Molly and Zeke jumped to their feet.

The lieutenant held out her hands, trying to calm them. "They're fine. All of them are well. But we're worried that the people targeting you might go after your family. They are being moved to a safe location. Your mother asked to be brought to her cousin's house in Pennsylvania. We need you to stay here, so we'll put you in a safe house until you're done. Then you'll join them."

She faced Zeke. "Mr. Bender, your brother will drive you back to your house tonight. Thank you for your help."

This was a nightmare. Her family had been shot at and were even now moving away from her. She was going into hiding on her own. And not even Zeke would be with her.

Did *Gott* no longer hear her?

SIX

Zeke shifted, looking as uncomfortable as she felt. For a moment, she thought he'd protest and ask to remain with her. She straightened. What was she doing? The last thing she wanted was to rely on a man, any man. If she was growing attached to him after a day in his presence, it would be intolerable if they stayed together.

Nee. She needed to be independent and allow him to leave with his brother as planned. When he opened his mouth, possibly to protest, she jumped in, cutting off whatever he had started to say.

"*Denke*, Lieutenant. That sounds like a *gut* plan." She turned to Zeke, fighting to keep her voice steady. "I'll be fine, Zeke. I appreciate all your help."

His eyes tightened. That was the only sign

he gave that her interruption distressed him. "*Ja.* I was glad to help. If you need me, you know where I live."

She could tell he wanted to say more. When he didn't, relief and disappointment fought for dominance in her head. She barely heard Micah when he spoke to her. Her whole focus remained on Zeke. He walked out of the room behind his brother, pausing at the doorway to glance at her, his blue eyes roaming her face. There was a question in that glance. She had no answer. Finally, he was gone.

What energy she'd had seemed to flee with his absence. She could no longer hold back a yawn. Her lids grew heavy and her arms seemed weighted down. The temptation to use the album in front of her on the table as a pillow pulled at her. Without thinking, she folded her arms and lay her head down, closing her eyes.

"I guess this is my hint that we're done for the night."

She jerked upright, her eyes suddenly wide open. Lieutenant Bartlett grinned at her, sympathy dancing in her gaze. "It's okay. You've had enough. We'll head out for the safe house.

Tomorrow, you can come back and begin again."

She pressed her lips together, holding the emotion battering inside her head at bay.

She wanted her life back. Her family had already been through so much, and now they were in the midst of yet another trial that she wasn't prepared to deal with. Hopelessness flooded her. Her eyes stung. She blinked rapidly, refusing to give in, no matter what. She had a reputation for being strong.

Except she wasn't. So often, she barely kept her head above the mounting pressures each day brought.

At moments like this, she wished she could still turn to *Gott*. Shame built inside her. She'd called on Him the other day. Had He listened? Her family had undergone a couple of attacks.

But they were alive.

Was that *Gott*? She'd always known suffering and life went together. But was He watching over her in the eye of the storm?

She couldn't think about that now. The breaking point was too near. She tried to sidestep it by turning her mind off.

"Miss Schultz?" One of the officers who'd

driven her to the police department earlier stood before her. "The chief wants us to escort you to the safe house for the night."

She nodded, too tired to respond. She was on autopilot now. Numbly, she followed them to the car. The officer who had spoken to her held the back door open for her. She stepped inside and sat, buckling herself in. He shut the door, and she stared out the window without seeing the landscape. Both officers got into the front seat. The car started, the low rumble of the vehicle had a soothing effect. She ignored the low conversation in the seat ahead of her. Her brain couldn't absorb one more detail. Soon, the motion lulled her to sleep. When the car jolted, she awoke to find they were already at the house. A marshal met them inside of it. He offered her something to eat. Molly shook her head. Her queasy stomach wouldn't keep anything down. Instead, she headed to the bedroom they directed her to. She lay down, fully dressed, intending to rest her weary soul and body for a few minutes. Closing her eyes, she drifted off to sleep.

Shouting woke her. Daylight streamed through the window. How long had she slept?

The clock on her bedside table read six-sixteen. She'd slept right through the night. But who was shouting and why?

A sharp crack and the sound of glass breaking had her scrambling off the bed. For a second, the aroma of smoke hovered on the air.

Was the building on fire?

Molly leaped from the bed and ran out in the hall. The police officer she'd talked with the night before grabbed her arm and yanked her out of the house, but not quick enough. Her shocked gaze took in two bodies draped across the furniture and lying on the floor, eyes wide open and staring.

The other officer and the marshal. Both dead.

"Come on! We have to move!" He tugged at her arm.

She stumbled behind him.

He dragged her out through the garage. She started to run toward the car parked in the bay. He yanked on her arm, pulling her to the back of the garage. "Not that car. It's a decoy."

She had no idea what he meant. When he ducked out the door leading to the backyard, she ran to keep up with him. They flew into the pole barn. He grabbed hold of a large black tarp covering a boxy object and tugged it off to reveal a second police cruiser.

They jumped in and he hit a button and the pole barn door opened. The cruiser shot through the door and barreled down the driveway, swinging wide as they turned onto the road.

"We'll go back to the police department," he informed her. She nodded, then listened as he called in the safe house breach. So many deaths. How many more people would die before they caught the people responsible? If they caught them. There was no guarantee they would.

"That's not good," the officer muttered, his gaze sliding to the rearview mirror.

She glanced at him sharply. "What now?"

"We're being followed."

She twisted in her seat. The SUV behind them wasn't familiar. It definitely wasn't the same vehicle that had chased her the day before. Micah and Steve had thought there was more than one person involved. This might prove it.

The cruiser sped up. The SUV kept up with it. She gasped when a gun of some sort poked out the window and barked. The side view mirror shattered. The young cop beside her perspired.

"I'm going to try to get you to the police department. If we need to stop, or if they catch up, you need to head north." He pointed at the glove compartment. "Grab the compass in there. It will always point north."

Her hand shook as she opened the door and grabbed a small compass. It looked like an old-fashioned pocket watch. She flipped it open and saw the little red arrow hovered on the *N*.

The car lurched forward. Molly screamed. They'd been rammed from behind. The cruiser took the hit on the driver's side near the rear wheel and the car spun out of control. It flew into the guardrail and stopped. The police officer yanked his gun from his holster and placed his hand on the door. Her window rolled down.

"When I get out, you run."

Then he was out of the car, firing at the SUV. She climbed and wiggled her way out of the window. When she looked back at him, he was already down. There was nothing she could do for him but honor his sacrifice. She ran.

The bullets came after her.

One of the men gave chase.

She kept going, listening to him huff and wheeze behind her. One glance over her shoulder proved her pursuer was slowing down. He was an older man, probably around the age her *daed* would have been if he were alive. With every step, the distance between them grew and she outpaced him. Still she ran. She had no way of knowing if he'd been alone in the car, or if his hypothetical passenger was in better shape than he was.

Molly shoved all thoughts and concerns deep down inside. She'd think later. Right now, her sole focus had to be surviving each minute. Her leg ached. Her side began to burn. She didn't stop. She couldn't.

Finally, she reached her limit. She slowed to a walk, limping in pain. Her stomach growled, reminding her she hadn't eaten since yesterday evening at her *haus*. Instantly, her mind flew to her family. Had they arrived at the cousin's *haus*? Her spirits sank lower than ever with the uncertainty.

Bowing her head, she gave in and prayed for guidance and for help, both for herself and her family. She prayed for the families who would suffer after losing a husband or father due to these horrible people who wouldn't stop searching for her. She prayed for the Stevens family, wondering if Terry was still alive, and for Deputy US Marshal Parker Gates. By the time she ran out of words, the top of her dress and her apron were damp from the drops falling off her chin. She had emptied her eyes and her heart.

She didn't feel empty, though. Incredibly, peace filled her bruised heart, soothing her wounded soul. *Gott* had heard her. She didn't know what would happen, but at least she knew He was there with her. It had been a long time.

She continued walking, checking her compass to make sure she continued journeying north. She hadn't asked their names, the officers who'd died for her. She regretted her self-absorption. If she ever had the opportunity, she'd make sure to let their families know how brave and honorable they'd been.

It was all the comfort she'd have to offer.

Suddenly, she paused, glancing around, frowning. She recognized where she was. They hadn't been as far from Sutter Springs as she'd imagined. In fact, if she continued walking, she might be able to get to the police station.

Nee, that would take over an hour by buggy.

But she could get to Zeke's *haus*. While they'd driven to her *haus*, she'd taken care to note which roads they were on. It wouldn't be an easy walk, but it would be more feasible than any other destination she could think of. Definitely not her *haus*. They'd find her for sure.

Tightening her jaw, she trudged on.

Zeke's *haus* it was.

Zeke stood near the horse's head, his back to the beast, and held the abscessed hoof between his knees to keep the leg steady. Careful not to hurt the mare, he dug out the infection, keeping up a steady stream of comforting words for the animal.

His *daed* always laughed when he listened to him talking to the animals. It was a habit he'd gotten into, though, and it no longer felt natural to work quietly when dealing with hurt animals.

Finally, he finished and let the hoof slide to the ground. The mare snorted and lipped the brim of his hat.

"You're *welkum*."

He wiped off the tool he'd used and turned

to the concerned stable manager. "You'll need to soak the infected hoof in warm water and Epsom salt," he informed her. "You don't want the infection to worsen. Also, you'll want to pack it."

He proceeded to instruct her on the proper care. Once satisfied that she understood the steps and their necessity, he packed up his equipment and loaded it back into Neil's van. In less than thirty minutes, he'd be back at his *haus* and faced with a long, relatively easy day. He had some tasks to complete at the workshop, and one more appointment later in the day. If he had time, he also needed to complete repairs on his farrier wagon. He'd gone long enough without it. He worked better when he didn't have to plan appointments around a driver. It would probably take him most of the afternoon to repair it.

Which meant he'd have no time to stand around wondering about Molly. How she was and if she was safe.

Sighing, he shut the back door and walked to the front of the van. Molly was no longer his responsibility. She had the police guarding her and they'd protect her family, too.

Micah had returned to his home, but he'd

told Zeke he'd be back if he was needed. Zeke appreciated how quickly his brother had responded the day before, but Molly and her family were now under the protection of the Sutter Springs Police Department. Plus, his brother had his own job and family to worry about.

He hopped up into the passenger seat of the van. Neil set his phone in the console and started the engine. He began the brief drive back to Zeke's *haus*. After a minute or so, he cleared his throat. "Hey, I know this is late notice, but I have a conflict this afternoon."

Zeke turned his head and frowned at his driver.

"This is the third time this month."

"Yeah, yeah. I know. It's not something I can help—"

Zeke forced himself not to scowl. Neil was normally dependable, but lately he'd been rather scattered. He'd called in several times, leaving Zeke in a tight spot. As much as he hated to put pressure on the other man, he had a business to run. He'd need to start searching for another driver for his regular appointments.

He tuned out the younger man's excuses.

He had an appointment this afternoon that he couldn't put off. If he couldn't find another driver, he'd have to hook up his mobile farrier work bench and haul it to the customer's *haus* himself. That wouldn't be his preference, but he might not have a choice. He sighed. Fixing his wagon was no longer something to do in his spare time. Now it was imperative that he make the repairs as soon as possible. He wouldn't have time to fix everything, but he could get it so it would be safe to use.

Neil made several attempts to talk, his voice full of forced joviality. Zeke responded, but his mind wasn't on the conversation. Finally, they fell silent. He sank deep into his own thoughts and they drifted back to Molly. If only he could reach out to her. Micah might be able to get him information, but he wouldn't put his brother in an awkward position.

After several strained minutes, he concluded he needed to be blunt. "Neil, I understand you have other priorities. You've been a wonderful *gut* driver, and I appreciate all your help. But I am running a business, ain't so? I will lose clients if I can't keep appointments. I need to know that I can depend on my driver. I think it's time I search for a new driver. At least for now."

He tacked on that last sentence to lessen the harshness. It didn't help. Neil's face hardened like he had cement under his skin. For a moment, his expression turned ugly, like a man capable of unthinkable acts. Instantly, Zeke's mind went to the image of Parker Gates bleeding on Molly's floor.

He glanced back at Neil. The expression had melted off his face, almost like it had never been there. Zeke wrestled with the possibility of whether or not Neil could have been involved. Granted, he was with Zeke when the first attack happened and sent Molly running, but he saw the yellow car. Had he talked to the driver? Zeke didn't remember. If he knew the driver, he might have asked for his help. What if he had seen Molly in the van?

He shook his head. *Nee*, Neil couldn't really be involved. It was a coincidence.

He still didn't want to hire him to drive again.

The van halted. Zeke startled. He hadn't noticed they'd arrived at his *haus*. He thanked Neil and hopped down from the van. It took five minutes to unload his equipment from the back of the vehicle, but it felt longer. Neil didn't attempt to talk to him, his mouth tight in a sullen line. Zeke tried to catch his eye twice, but that didn't work, either. Neil never raised his head enough to look him in the face.

While he felt bad, Zeke wouldn't give in and try to placate him. Maybe if Neil realized he couldn't back out on clients and keep their loyalty, he'd make better choices in the future. As the younger man returned to his spot behind the steering wheel, Zeke determined to remain pleasant. It wasn't his fault the other man was upset.

"*Denke* for helping me with the equipment." Zeke stepped away from the van. Neil needed space to maneuver.

The friendly man he'd contracted with for months grunted and glared, his face screwed into an angry mask.

Zeke stared back, keeping all expression from his face. When one faced an angry dog ready to strike, it was best to keep calm and not make any sudden moves. Or so he'd heard. And right now, Neil looked angry enough to run him down with that vehicle.

He jerked the vehicle into Reverse and

slammed his foot down on the gas pedal. The van flew out of the driveway backward, kicking up dirt, dust and gravel, then screeched forward and zoomed away.

That was the last time he'd hire Neil, even if the man did become more reliable. He didn't need to work with someone with that kind of explosive temper. He frowned. Up until an hour ago, he would have said Neil was a pleasant young man who was always willing to lend a hand. He obviously didn't know the man as well as he'd thought he did.

He didn't have a *gut* history of judging people. His wife. Neil. He was sick and tired of being surprised when someone wasn't who he thought they were. But was it his fault? He had loved Iris, but on some level, he wondered if he avoided looking too deep into the character of the people who surrounded him. Frustrated, he spun away from the dust shimmering in the air where his former driver had just been and stalked toward the workshop. He had too many items to tick off his list today and couldn't afford indulging in self-recriminations. *Gott* would provide. He always had.

An hour later, his optimism faded. He'd

called every driver on his list. Not one of them had been available this afternoon. This particular appointment required his attention today and could not be put off until tomorrow or the next day. Which meant repairing the farrier wagon needed to be his priority once he returned home. He'd have to hook it up and drive himself there. He would have to start earlier than planned. The rest of the day's tasks needed to be rearranged to fit this new complication.

He scowled. He would have been fine if Neil hadn't had a conflict.

Although, maybe this would be a blessing. At least now, he'd had a glimpse into who Neil truly was in his heart.

He completed as many chores as he could before the time arrived to get ready to depart for his appointment. He loaded all the tools he might need, making sure they were clean and in *gut* working condition. Zeke took pains to never appear unprepared in front of a client.

He hitched his mare to the wagon. Checking all the fittings to make sure they were tight enough, he placed his right foot on the step in the front of the wagon.

Wait. He'd left his receipt ledger in the *haus*.

Jumping away from the wagon, he jogged to the office door and hurried inside to grab the ledger. He made sure he had a couple of pens, too.

Someone knocked on the office door. He furrowed his brow. He hadn't seen anyone outside. Nor had he heard anyone pull into the driveway.

Carefully, he walked to the window and peered outside.

His heart thumped in his chest.

Molly Schultz stood on his porch, looking scared, bruised and defeated.

What had happened since he'd last seen her?

SEVEN

Molly shivered, although she wasn't cold.

Standing on Zeke's porch, anyone would see her if they passed the *haus*. Shifting closer to the closed door for protection, she crossed her arms across her body to try to control their shaking. She half expected someone to charge up the driveway, yelling. Or maybe they'd have a gun pointed at her. Or maybe they'd throw a knife at her. Or—

The door flew open. She screamed.

Her scream was muffled against someone's shoulder. Zeke. She relaxed in his strong arms. He hustled her into the *haus* and pushed the door closed with one hand. The other one remained around her, holding her close. Her breath exploded from her in a sob. She was safe. No one had caught up with her. Pressing her forehead closer to Zeke, she inhaled.

The familiar scent of him calmed her. For a moment she allowed herself to nestle in his arms. Then, the reality of her position caught up with her. What was she doing?

Heat swirled in her cheeks. She untangled herself from his embrace and moved back, her gaze avoiding his. She'd never dissolved in Aaron's arms the way she'd done with Zeke, and she'd been planning a wedding with Aaron. Zeke was practically a stranger. She couldn't fathom the way she reacted to him. Or how quickly she'd grown to trust him, to depend on him. It wasn't healthy.

As soon as she could get back to the police station, she'd leave Zeke to his life again. It would be better for them both. But until then, she had to protect her heart and not get attached.

"Molly? I don't understand. The police were bringing you to a safe haus. How are you here?"

"I ran most of the way." Exhaustion hit her and she could barely force the words out.

His jaw dropped open. She might have enjoyed his shock if she weren't worn-out and mentally overwhelmed.

"You ran."

Suddenly the reality of all she'd seen that

day hit her with the force of a brick wall smashing down on her. Her legs folded, unable to hold her weight any longer. She crumpled but didn't drop to the floor. Zeke was there, his arms once more catching her. He lifted her and carried her to the padded chair at his desk. He set her on it like she was fragile and would shatter at any moment. Maybe she would.

For a minute, he left her. She had no energy to call him back. So, she waited. He returned with a glass of water and handed it to her. She needed both hands to hold it steady. Lifting the glass, she sipped the water. It was barely cool, not ice-cold like she preferred it. It was the best water she'd ever had. Feeling stronger, she drank deeply, draining the glass. When it was empty, she handed it back to him and wiped her mouth.

"*Denke*. I didn't realize I was so thirsty."

He set the glass aside. "If you've been running, it makes sense. You're dehydrated. I can see your tongue is white."

She nodded. She hadn't had anything to drink since they'd been at the police station the day before.

"Tell me what happened."

She closed her eyes. "I fell asleep as soon

as we reached the safe *haus*. I slept through the night. This morning, one of the officers, I never learned his name, woke me and forced me to leave the *haus*. I saw the other two officers who were there. I'm pretty sure they were both dead."

"Dead! Are you sure?" he exclaimed. She nodded, but she pressed on. If she didn't finish the narrative now, she doubted she'd ever get it out. Bile rose in her throat. She swallowed. She had to continue.

"We got out and made it to a car. I thought we were okay, but then we were followed. They crashed into the back of our car, and we were stuck. The officer gave me a compass, told me to head north, then faced the killers. He was shot, and I ran. Maybe I should have stayed..."

"Absolutely not! You did the right thing."

She barely paused at his exclamation. "I was chased, but I got away because I'm faster. When I realized I was close to your *haus*, I headed here. I'm sorry. I don't want to be an inconvenience. But you were my only hope."

She leaned her head back against the chair and opened her eyes. Would he blame her? Steeling herself, she lifted her gaze to his face, expecting to see disapproval. Instead, she met compassion.

"You were very brave," he whispered.

"Brave?" She shook he head, biting her lips to still their trembling. "I don't feel brave. In fact, I feel the complete opposite. I left that officer and ran. And the other officers, the ones back at the *haus*? They are dead because of me. If they didn't have to protect me, they would go home to their families."

She'd finally voiced it, the fear roiling around in her soul.

Zeke dropped into a squat in front of her, his hands on the arms of the chair. She reared back at the sudden movement, then relaxed.

"I want to tell you a story. I told you my wife died, *ja*?"

She nodded, recalling that conversation.

"Iris had a younger brother, Danny. Someone told her they'd kill Danny if she didn't do something. Something wrong, which she knew would lead to someone else getting hurt. Maybe killed. Instead of informing me, or trying to find another way, she agreed."

Molly covered her mouth with one hand, appalled.

"Well, Iris was shot and killed before it

ended." He lowered his head, a huge sigh escaping him. "I blamed myself for so long. After all, I was her husband. She should have *cumme* to me. But she didn't. I have finally started to see that I am not responsible for her choices. Just as you are not responsible for the choices of the men doing these evil things."

"So, I should forgive myself?"

"*Ja.* You can't make decisions for other people. All you can do is make your own decisions based on what is right. And pray, of course."

Molly froze. "I haven't been very *gut* at praying lately."

Zeke didn't respond. Neither did he back away, repulsed. He waited for her to continue.

"After the accident, it was so hard to move on. My *daed* was gone, and so was my fiancé. My *mamm* would never walk again, and Caleb is still in a coma. The doctors don't know if he'll ever wake up. I'm terrified they'll tell us we have to make a decision and remove him from the machines. Or that the bishop will decide this is too extraordinary. Then what? I felt like *Gott* didn't hear me anymore."

"*Ach.* He hears you, Molly. I know it's hard. We struggled after my sister disappeared. It seemed so cruel. No matter how hard we prayed, she wasn't found."

He pushed himself up and moved to lean against the desk. She missed the closeness.

"But I've been thinking," he continued. "*Gott* knew what would happen. I'm reminded of the story in the Bible. The one where Joseph tells his brothers that they meant to do evil, but *Gott* used it for *gut*. Maybe our sufferings are like that."

She searched his honest face. There was no doubt he understood suffering and death. He knew about blame and about watching those he loved suffer.

"What happened with Isaiah?" She hadn't meant to blurt it out like that.

The skin around his eyes and mouth tightened. If she could erase the words she would. But they sat between them now.

The breath stalled in his lungs.

He hadn't heard anyone outside the family say Isaiah's name in years. It was almost as if his younger brother had been erased from the fabric of their lives. But he knew it wasn't so. Although they were careful not to do so in their parents' hearing, he and his other siblings had all discussed Isaiah. It was hard not to wonder where he was now.

Zeke refused to believe his brother was dead.

It had been twelve years since he'd last seen or heard from him.

"We don't talk about him much," he finally choked out.

"I'm sorry. I shouldn't have asked."

Suddenly, seeing the apology on her face, he found he wanted to talk about his brother. He wanted her to know.

"It's all right. Isaiah, like Micah and I, blamed himself for our sister's disappearance."

Her head wagged back and forth, a fierce expression stamped on her face. "You were a *kind*. It wasn't your fault."

"*Ja*. I know that. But it's hard to convince your mind of something when your heart believes the opposite. Ain't so?"

"*Ja*." She sighed. "That's true."

She would know.

"Anyway, Isaiah always kept things close. He wasn't one to share feelings or talk things out."

"Like you?"

He blinked. He hadn't thought she saw him

that way. "Not exactly. I will discuss feelings if there's a conversation or need to do so. Isaiah closed up tighter than a clam whenever emotions or personal topics arose. Something happened when he was seventeen. A friend of his died. It wasn't his fault, but it broke him. He left the community, and we haven't heard from him in over a decade. It weighs wonderful heavy on *Mamm* and *Daed*."

She didn't say anything for a moment. Her brows scrunched. "How do they deal with all the heartache?"

"They have their faith. It also helps that they were able to forgive those that hurt them."

Her head shot up. "Forgiveness. I'm not there yet."

He hesitated, not sure he was the best person to advise her.

"Have you forgiven your wife?"

And there it was. He puffed air through his teeth and blew out a hard breath. "I'm working on it."

How awful it sounded. He hadn't forgiven his wife, even though she was dead. Internally squirming, he glanced up at the clock on the wall. Seeing the time, he recalled his schedule and bounded to his feet.

"I have an appointment. I'm already late."

All the color drained from her face. She thought he'd leave her behind. There was no way he'd abandon her. Not after everything she'd been through.

"I couldn't find a driver, so I've hitched my farrier wagon to my mare. She's been waiting for me outside. If it's all right with you, we'll go and take care of my client. Then when we're done, we'll be halfway to town, so we'll continue on to the police department."

She quirked an eyebrow. "Can't you call your brother or your brother-in-law?"

"*Nee*, unfortunately. Steve's at court all day and Micah is on a field op in another county. We'll be better off going to the station."

Carefully, she placed her feet on the floor and stood, almost as if she expected to topple over again. "If you're sure I won't be in the way, I'll *cumme*."

She was the bravest woman he'd ever met. She might not see it that way, but the fact that she'd remain behind, regardless of her own terror and misgivings, said a lot about her character. The urge to step closer and kiss her stunned him. They weren't walking out, or dating. Where had that desire *cumme* from?

He stared a little too long while trying to collect his thoughts and rein in his inappropriate urge. Her face flushed and those gorgeous blue eyes dropped in confusion.

"Of course, you won't be in the way. *Cumme.* We need to go."

He couldn't explain what had really been in his thoughts. Pretending not to feel the sudden tension between them, he gathered his ledger again and headed toward the door. A few seconds later, he smiled when her softer footfalls echoed behind him. *Gut.* She had decided to trust him. He grabbed his hat off the hook near the door and shoved it on his head.

Dear Lord, help me live up to her trust.

Outside, the bright blue sky had changed and become partly cloudy. The clouds weren't heavy yet—nothing to worry about. They moved swiftly across the sky. Hopefully, they'd be back before they became heavier or turned to rain. If only Neil hadn't bailed on him.

But if he hadn't, Zeke might not have been home when Molly showed up on his porch. She'd been so scared. *Nee*, he'd rather be a bit inconvenienced than leave her to face this trial alone.

Helping her to sit on the handmade bench, he settled beside her and urged the mare forward with a flick of his wrist.

"I've never seen a farrier wagon like this before." Molly half turned on her seat, surveying the equipment stored behind them.

"I made this one." He did his best to keep pride from his voice. It was difficult. He'd designed it himself and had built it in his spare time. "It was damaged in a storm, but I spent a few hours today getting it ready enough to use."

"It's lovely."

Lovely wasn't the word he'd have used, but he appreciated the sentiment. He flicked the reins, urging the mare into a trot.

When he brought the wagon to a halt in front of his client's barn, Preacher Levi Hostetler strode out to greet them, a ready smile on his bearded face.

"Zeke! I expected a van. Although, you know me. I get a kick out of seeing new inventions. I've been wanting to see this new wagon you've built for months."

Molly's eyebrows wiggled as if she was forcibly holding them down, keeping them from rising. He was surprised. Didn't she know Levi? He was a preacher in her district, not his. She waved at the preacher with familiarity. Ah. She was probably surprised he had hired Zeke. Zeke wasn't proud, but he knew he had a solid reputation for doing quality work at a fair price.

Levi glanced at her. "Molly! It's *gut* to see you."

"Levi," Molly greeted him. "How are Lilah and the *kinder*?"

Levi's grin grew. "They are *gut*. Harrison will start school this fall."

They chatted for a few minutes. When Levi returned to the *haus* to tend to some business, Zeke asked her why she'd seemed so surprised to see him.

"I wasn't expecting my best friend's cousin to be your client. Also, Levi is a bit outrageous, but he's a wonderful *gut* preacher."

"So, I've heard."

Zeke began setting up his equipment. He worked quickly trimming the hooves of both of Preacher Levi's horses. The mare stood still, used to his touch. The colt, however, hadn't decided if he liked Zeke playing with his feet. It took several tries and two escapes before the job was completed to his satisfaction.

Molly and Levi were both standing near the barn door, grinning, by the time he was done.

He set about cleaning up.

"Want help?"

He smiled at Molly. "*Denke, nee.* I have a specific way I do this. I'll be ready to leave in five minutes."

It was closer to seven, but she didn't comment.

By the time they were traveling once more, the clouds had grown heavier in the sky. It was *gut* that he had secured his tools and covered them with a tarp.

"It's going to rain for sure," he mused. "We might get wet on the way to the station."

He didn't mention the ride home. He had no doubt she'd be with the police again and he'd be making the return trip solo. The idea dimmed his spirits. He would worry every moment she was out of his sight, but he knew he wasn't the one to protect her. She needed to be with people who had the means to withstand an assault.

He recalled that she'd had three officers protecting her earlier and all had been killed. Only the *Gut Gott* had gotten her to his home safely. No other explanation accounted for how she came to be there, alive and un-harmed.

An engine revved in the distance. Frowning, Zeke narrowed his gaze and scanned the horizon for oncoming vehicles. He didn't see any, but cold fingers wrapped around his heart. Next to him, Molly stirred and rubbed her hands on her apron. A moment later, she shifted closer to him.

"We need to get off this road," he said.

"How? There are no paths."

He glanced around. She was correct. There were no paths. And the horse would not be able to cross the ditch with the wagon in tow. He couldn't rescue her and the wagon both. Neither would he leave the mare defenseless.

"Maybe we can turn around and go back to Levi's."

He nodded. It was worth a try. They started to turn the wagon. They were too close to the ditch, though. The mare backed up and then started forward, but one of the wheels hung over the edge.

"Zeke!" He turned.

A yellow car was coming. He'd only ever seen one car that color. "Molly, jump! Get into the ditch!"

EIGHT

"Don't worry about me," Zeke hollered when she hesitated. "Go!"

Zeke watched her leap off into the ditch. He slithered off his side as the car zoomed toward them. He didn't have time to save the wagon. It was stuck *gut*, and he couldn't risk it. Running to the front, he unhitched the mare, then swatted her rear to get her moving.

The horse took off to the other side of the road and into the field. She'd be fine.

He sprinted to the back and dived into the ditch next to Molly. Tugging her hand, he pulled her along. They needed to move. They'd only run a few steps when the car smashed into the wagon. Wood and metal crunched together with a horrendous smash. Zeke shuddered. The desire to stop and turn back and see how badly the farrier wagon was destroyed nearly overwhelmed him, but he refused to give in. Right now, even a second wasted on something as trivial as the wagon was a second too many. Molly's life depended on them getting away quickly.

The car that had come after them backed up. He could hear the engine revving. Smoke and the smell of burned rubber were thick in the air. He didn't think it was possible for the car to jump the ditch and come after them, but he pulled Molly faster just in case. Even if the man didn't come after them in the car, there was still the chance he could shoot at them or hit them with a flying knife, the way he had Parker Gates. Zeke was taking no chances.

The air rent with a sudden pop and a loud hiss.

Molly glanced over her shoulder and gasped. "His tire blew. He must've run over something."

"Keep going. We need to go as fast as we can before he gets started after us on foot."

Fortunately, Zeke knew the area they were in by heart. He'd grown up in these parts. He knew the trees, he knew the woods and he knew who wouldn't mind them crossing through their backyard and who would. Specifically, he knew who owned a fierce guard dog and who didn't.

Leading Molly, he wove their way through backyards. Several of the yards had tall fences. They avoided those if they could. One of the yards, though, they had to go through.

"I'll never be able to get over the fence," Molly's voice whispered in his ear.

He agreed. But they had to go through this one and the next. Otherwise, they'd be walking along the street, and they couldn't do that. Behind the houses the terrain angled sharply. Not quite a cliff, but steep enough that you had to be careful not to twist your ankle or fall clear off the thing. It was at least a thirty-foot drop. And you would land on the sharp rocks below. A few decades back, the previous owners had undertaken the task of building a path with steps down the side of the incline. No one ever used it, though. It was far too steep and treacherous. They couldn't cut through the yard, though, without alerting the residents, or their dog would attack them.

"Maybe we can knock on the door and they'll let us through," he speculated. He doubted it, though; the people who lived here guarded their privacy to an extreme. They never let anyone into their house, not even to use the telephone.

"Why can't we walk down there?" Molly pointed at the drop-off. From where they stood, the first two steps were visible.

"It's really steep. I think it would be difficult to walk." Close to impossible, actually.

Molly shrugged and wandered to the edge to look down. "I don't think it looks that bad."

Zeke opened his mouth to protest, determined to make her see reason, but the sound of heavy footsteps tromping after them changed his mind. They were out of time, which meant they were out of options.

Running over to Molly, he motioned for her to follow him. "I don't like this path, but I know where it leads. It's narrow, but the one side is against the side of the hill, like a wall. If we stay close to the walls, we will be all right."

He tried to sound more confident than he felt. The last time he'd been on this path, he'd been all of fifteen years old, and had thought he was invincible. One hike along it with a friend had convinced him that he was as mortal as anyone else. He'd firmly declined all invitations to hike on it since that awful day sixteen years ago.

"The trick is to stay as close to the wall as you can."

She promised, her face a lot less confident than it had been when she'd glibly said they should use the path.

The steps against the side of the hill were uneven and a few were coated with moss. It had probably seemed like a *gut* idea to build them right up against the side of the hill so people could walk to the bottom of the cliff-like formation and hike the forest floor. He said as much to her as they approached the first steps.

She looked at him, one eyebrow quirked in doubt. "I can't imagine why anyone would think that was a *gut* idea."

He had to agree. The trail was bad enough. The steps were nothing short of treacherous. Steep, they were made of some kind of granite that became slippery when wet. The fact that they were uneven and narrow didn't help. Maybe if the mastermind behind the trail had included a rail it wouldn't have been so dangerous. As it was, one missed step could lead someone to tumble over the side.

They probably wouldn't die. They'd be in a world of hurt, though. He couldn't imagine anyone falling over and not breaking something.

Molly had a limp from the injuries she'd incurred during the accident that had devastated her family. Would that make it difficult for her to navigate the trail?

"Keep a hand on my shoulder if you need to," he whispered over his shoulder. That way, if she stumbled, she could catch herself on him. He was fairly certain he could steady them before they went over.

When her small hand settled on his shoulder, he had to remind himself what they were doing. He'd never imagined helping a neighbor would prove to be so distracting. In fact, he had believed Iris's death had killed his ability to find another woman intriguing.

He'd been wrong.

Focusing on his steps, he lowered himself one step at a time, trying to take into account her shorter stride.

It took them ten minutes, but finally they reached the end of the steps and began to move along the trail that ran parallel to the houses on the block. They had only gone half a dozen steps before Zeke held up his hands, silently telling Molly to stop.

He motioned for her to stand still as close to the wall as she could. She nodded once, then obediently flattened herself against the rock. Zeke did the same.

A few feet above them, the distinct sound of boots crunching along the dirt in the backyard drifted down to them. It could have been anyone. It could have been the owners of the *haus*, or it could have been one of the neighborhood kids trespassing. But he knew it wasn't. In his heart, he knew the man who had smashed his farrier wagon was above them.

Beside him, Molly worried her bottom lip with her teeth, her face white. She remained motionless otherwise. Even when she met his glance, nothing moved but the irises of her eyes.

Did the killer know they were down there? Zeke really hadn't thought the man would be familiar with this territory like he was. Perhaps that was hubris. Maybe he should have assumed the man would have equal knowledge of the landscape. Now, if the killer started down the steps, they would be trapped and would have no alternative except to keep surging forward.

He forced the thoughts away so he could

concentrate on listening to what was happening above. After a few moments, the noises faded. Apparently, the killer had walked away from the edge.

He moved his head so he could whisper directly into her ear. Her warmth threatened to overwhelm him. "We can keep going, but let's go slow to keep the noise down."

She shivered. He hadn't thought it was cold. It was cooler in the shade, but maybe she was just reacting to the situation. Anyone would.

He reached out and gripped her hand, squeezing it for a moment in a silent show of support and understanding. He dropped it but not before he felt her shiver again.

A light dawned in his mind. Could it be—

He shook his head to push the thought away. Now was not the time to consider the implications of her reaction to him. It was probably all coincidence. But if it wasn't? They were facing the possibility of a killer catching up with them. Setting his jaw, he turned and began making his way along the path again.

A rapid tussle in the grass above them startled him. He motioned to Molly. They needed to quicken their pace. He heard a woman yell and a man shout.

The homeowners. He paused for a moment, unsure what to do. He hated to leave them in danger. Their pursuer was a cold-blooded murderer. They were a middle-aged couple with a sour attitude who rarely left their home. To his knowledge, they didn't have anything to use against intruders. He debated for a second longer until he heard the man give a single order.

"Attack, Daisy."

A bone-chilling canine growl echoed in the sudden silence, followed by a curse and the sound of a man rushing back toward the way they'd come. Daisy barked a few times.

Relieved, he grinned over his shoulder at Molly. "Daisy?" she whispered.

He nodded. He'd found it incongruous, as well. A sweet, cute little name given to an obviously vicious and efficient guard dog. They continued along the path for another five minutes. When they rested for a moment, he chuckled.

"If I ever have a daughter," he said on a laugh, "I might have to name her Daisy."

She smiled, but it seemed a bit pinched.

"How much farther?" she asked.

"Not far. Maybe another ten minutes. Then we'll be close enough to my *haus*. We'll be there soon. Then I can call my brother when he's done with court."

Wearily, she agreed, and they set out again. They'd been walking for a while before she broke the silence.

"It's getting wonderful dark. And I think it's colder than it was when we left Preacher Levi's *haus*."

Zeke glanced at the sky. Through the line of trees, he could barely make out the skyline. "It's cloudy. It looks like rain is on the way."

She sighed. He smiled. Her sigh was so heavy, he practically felt it on his neck.

"You don't like rain?"

This time she snorted, and he couldn't hold back a soft chuckle. She was adorable.

"I like rain fine, when I'm inside my cozy *haus* and can watch it from the windows. I also like to listen to the rain, from *inside*." She emphasized the last word.

He started to say he didn't mind the rain, but a fat drop landed on his nose, followed quickly by another.

She groaned. "Great. Now we're stuck in the rain, too."

"*Cumme*. We need to keep moving. Once

we're at my *haus*, I'll build a fire in the stove and you can dry off."

"It's July," she reminded him while she walked behind him.

"*Ja*. But you'll be wet. It will be *gut* to get you dry."

She didn't comment, just kept trudging along behind him. It seemed to take an hour, but eventually, they stepped off the trail and found themselves on a one-lane dirt road.

"Where are we?" She gazed around them, perplexed. "I thought I knew Sutter Springs well, but I don't know this road at all."

"Not many people do. This road used to be private property. When the owner died, the state took over the estate. The township started to build a road, intending to use it for some businesses, but then they never finished. So, it's an unnamed road with a dead end. We can cut through the property without fear of any owners siccing their dogs on us. My *haus* is straight through a few blocks."

"I can't wait for this to be over and done with." She nearly skipped up beside him. "I will never grouse at Abigail again about her haphazard cooking. Nor will I mind helping Betty with her math homework."

He cut his eyes toward her. "You don't like math."

"*Ach*. I like it fine. It was my favorite subject in school. Betty hates it. I keep trying new ways to teach it to her, but she says why bother? She won't need math as an adult."

"Of course, she will!"

"Right? She gets stubborn."

He almost offered to tutor the *kind*. Numbers had always made sense to Zeke. Sometimes more than people. He enjoyed helping others understand their complexities. But helping Betty would mean staying involved with Molly. And even if he didn't mind risking his heart by sticking around the feisty blonde, he wasn't sure she was interested in him.

Soon, she thought to herself. Soon she'd be warm. Zeke would call his brother, and all would be well. Micah would take care of everything. Maybe she'd even be able to sleep in her own bed tonight. Molly was a planner. She liked knowing what was happening in the immediate future. These past two days had been frustrating in the extreme. Not only was someone trying to kill her, and her family had to leave to go to a safe place, but also now she didn't know what was going to happen next. At some point, she knew she had to get into the police station and finish looking at images to help identify the man who was coming after them. She had no idea when that was going to happen.

And now it was raining.

Molly hadn't been kidding when she told Zeke that she liked the rain when she was inside. She didn't mean to sound ungrateful, but getting wet and cold and wearing a soggy prayer *kapp* would never be on her list of favorite things to do.

She bit her lip to keep from complaining. Zeke didn't have to help her. There was nothing in it for him. In fact, it was just the opposite. If he hadn't helped her, he'd still know where his trusted mare was and his farrier wagon would still be in one piece, rather than smashed into a jillion bits and pieces.

He hadn't flinched or hesitated. When the killer had come at them, Zeke's instinct had been to ensure she and the animal were safe. He hadn't even looked back to check on it once they started out across the field. As if it were nothing but a piece of equipment instead of something he'd taken hours, possibly days, to design and build.

They left the cover of the trees and started down the open road. Instantly, raindrops pitter-pattered on her *kapp*. Within a minute, the *kapp* was soaked and hung limply on her head. She might as well have put a wet dishrag over her hair.

Five minutes later, the skies opened up and the rain fell in torrents. Within moments, her boots made squelching noises as she walked. She'd meant to replace them but had needed the money for something else. Water seeped into the leaking soles and drenched her socks. She couldn't remember the last time she'd been this cold. It seemed to emanate from her bones. Her teeth chattered so hard her jaw ached.

"Here we are," Zeke said.

She lifted her head and saw the top of his barn come into view, followed by his *haus* and workshop. She had begun to doubt they would arrive in one piece. She stiffened her neck and jaw to ward off the onslaught of emotions rushing to break through.

"We'll go into my *haus* first. I'll build up a fire and we can dry off. I'll feed you, too."

Her stomach grumbled in response. She was too hungry, tired and cold to feel embarrassed. "That sounds perfect."

She had leaden weights for feet. She dragged them on the ground as they crossed to the *haus*. Plus, her leg ached something awful. She hoped he had some kind of pain reliever in his *haus*. Normally, she didn't bother with over-the-counter medicines. Rarely had she suffered pain that warmth and rest wouldn't heal. But in this instance, she didn't know how long she'd have access to either. She'd take the medicine so if they needed to travel again, she wouldn't hinder Zeke.

Another thought zipped across her mind, blindsiding her. Zeke had no reason to continue tagging along. Once he called his brother, she'd be off his hands. Whether she liked it or not, this was most likely the end of their short partnership.

She didn't like it. But she had nothing to say about it. Zeke didn't belong in this mess. He was only a *Gut* Samaritan, offering his aid to one in need. Other than helping her today, he had no further commitment to her.

She couldn't let herself forget that fact.

They crossed the threshold, and he immediately set to building a fire while she stood numbly, not knowing what to do.

He was a man she could easily fall in love

with, if she let herself forget to protect her heart. From now on, she had to be on her guard. She was grateful, though. Zeke had shaken her out of her cocoon, shown her that faith in the midst of trials was possible, and even beneficial. It was time she started investing herself in her relationship with *Gott*, instead of calling on him only in her time of need.

"Molly, *cumme*. I've built a fire."

She didn't need coaxing. She stood in front of the fire and held out her hands; it was barely warm yet, but it would get hotter soon. If she were home by herself or with her family, she'd remove her *kapp* and let her hair dry out, too.

She flushed at the idea of doing so. Only a husband saw a woman's hair. That was something Zeke would never be to her. She ignored the kernel of envy blooming inside her heart at the idea he might marry someone else.

Molly turned so he couldn't see her red face. She had no claim on him. It was difficult pretending she hadn't experienced an earth-shattering epiphany while standing in his living room and dripping on his wooden floor. He didn't appear to notice anything different, so she must have succeeded.

He moved a couple of chairs and two portable diner trays in front of the fire.

"I can set those up." She took the trays from him and opened them up. They were wood, and the legs formed a wide base. When they were set up, she tested them by pushing them lightly with her fingers and was pleased when they didn't wobble. They were wonderful sturdy.

Zeke had gone into the kitchen. She could hear him working. A few minutes later, he returned. He had made them a couple of sandwiches and cut up some cheese and some fruit for supper. They sat in their chairs and bowed their heads, silently giving thanks for the food. Then they both dug in to the meal. It was simple, but she was so hungry, it tasted like an expensive feast. She sipped the hot coffee he set in front of her without complaint.

Molly never drank coffee. She loathed the bitterness, and her *mamm* had never seen the point of fixing a beverage if you were going to add cream and sugar or other flavorings. So, at their *haus*, it was black coffee or water. It warmed her on the inside, so she choked down half a cup before setting it aside.

"Molly, your boots are soaked through!" Zeke exclaimed.

"*Ja.* I have a leak in them. I'll need to buy new ones before winter."

"You need new ones now. You can't wear these."

She raised her eyebrows. "I don't have a choice."

He frowned. "Wait here."

He pivoted on his heel and disappeared down the hall. She shrugged and faced the fire again. Her dress was nearly dry. She was almost warm. Soon, he'd go over and call his brother. Her stomach clenched. She'd have to relive the horror of the day.

Worse than that in her mind, this very day three families would learn the fates of their loved ones. She wanted to weep for the unfairness of it all. Instead, she drew in a deep breath, fortifying herself, and then she silently prayed for the families. It felt *gut* lifting others up to *Gott.*

Zeke returned, a pair of women's boots in his hands. Her eyes widened. They were prettier than Amish women normally wear. And they had heels. Why would Zeke's late wife have boots like those?

For a moment, revulsion filled her. She couldn't wear his dead wife's boots. She'd rather be cold.

"These are my sister's, but Joss won't mind you wearing them. She's a size seven."

So was she.

"Joss? Unusual name."

"She wasn't raised Amish. It's short for Josslyn."

He handed her the boots and a pair of socks. "I'll go call my brother while you put these on."

He fled the room, leaving her privacy. She literally had to peel the socks off her feet. Her toes resembled pale raisins from being wet for so long. Quickly, before he came back, she pulled on the dry socks and the pretty boots. She'd return them at the first opportunity.

Zeke rushed into the room. "We have to go. Out the back door. Quickly."

"Zeke—"

"The killer's in my workshop."

The breath whooshed out of her lungs. He had figured out that she was with Zeke. Her presence in his life had put him in danger.

NINE

"Don't even think it," Zeke ordered, seeing the look on her face. He grabbed her hand and tugged her to the back door. "This is not your fault. We need to move. Keep your head down."

She nodded but didn't say anything. At least she followed his directions. Now was not the time for conversation. They needed to flee. He didn't know how he'd contact his brother, or how he'd get her to the police. His best chance would be to find someone to give them a ride into town.

Outside, the rain continued to pour down. Their recently dried clothing would be soaked in no time. Thankfully, she had better boots and socks to keep her feet warm and dry. At the door, he handed her an overlarge rain slicker. Then he slipped another one over his own clothing. He kept several around for when he needed to go see a horse in inclement weather.

Grabbing her hand, he tugged her out of the *haus* and toward the barn. Inside, they ducked into one of the empty stalls.

"Why aren't we leaving?" she breathed, her words mere whispers of sound.

"I couldn't tell if he was alone," he replied. "His car was idling on the side of the road, and I could see someone moving from inside the *haus.*"

"I didn't think the car still worked."

He flinched, thinking of his farrier wagon, crushed to bits, and his mare. The horse should find her way home. It wouldn't surprise him if he saw her in the field when they left the barn. She was as faithful an animal as they came. "I didn't think it could, either. Obviously, we were wrong. He must have changed the tire, though."

They quieted as a door slammed shut. That was closer than the workshop. They had entered the *haus.* If he hadn't gone to call his brother, they might have been caught unawares. He shuddered. It was almost seven in the evening. The rain had not let up, and at least one killer was searching his *haus* for her. For them. He wasn't leaving her again until this situation was solved.

What if they checked the barn? If he were intent on finding someone or something, he would check every building in the area. "We can't stay here."

"I thought you said we can't go out in the street."

"We can't. We need to find a different way out." He thought for a moment. "Follow me. And stay down. My guess is they will search for us here next."

"I'm sorry."

He shook his head. "Like I said before, it is not your fault if evil men make evil choices. They are to blame. Not you. And not me."

He edged his way toward the back of the barn. Once he was reasonably sure no one was nearby, he led her out the door. The rain continued to fall. Streams of water ran off the overhangs of the barn, creating puddles near the walls.

"I'm glad you are wearing Joss's boots," he whispered. Then winced. What had happened to him? He used to be the quiet brother, the one who rarely spoke. He had grown almost verbose these past couple days, to the point where he was blurting out random thoughts. He peered down at Molly, chagrined. She held a finger to her lips and shushed him. He nodded. She was right. Did he see a speck of humor in her gaze? Surely not.

He looked back at the *haus*. As he had expected, the man who had been traipsing through his office and then his *haus* entered the barn. He spied another figure sitting in the car. He felt like a sitting duck, standing out here while killers searched his *haus*. He scanned the area, searching for a way out that wouldn't wind up with them getting killed.

Molly had said another man, an older man, had chased her after she left the safe *haus*. Was he in the car, waiting for his partner? Zeke shuddered to consider the possibility that there may have been more than two villains after her. What could motivate men to do such awful deeds?

The answer came swiftly. Money. Greed was a motivator like no other. For those who desired money or power, what they had was never enough. He didn't understand the craving for material possessions himself. Nothing in his life was more important than his faith or his family.

The question was, who was paying and why. Had it been a drug deal that Molly had walked into that day? His brother would be better able to answer the question. Once he was finally able to contact Micah, he'd ask just that.

The car door opened and the man stepped outside. He ducked his head between his shoulders and ran with loud, splashy steps to barn, holding a newspaper over his head. Had he not been so concerned about the rain, he might have spotted them.

"Let's move on while he is in the barn." Zeke kept his voice to a whisper, not wanting anyone to overhear.

Molly gave him a thumbs-up. As they crept along the fence by the pasture, he heard a low nicker. Lifting his head at the familiar sound, his heart warmed. His mare had returned safely, just as he had hoped she would. He had no idea how long he and Molly would be on the run. Hopefully, they would be able to return very soon. If not, the horse would be able to eat sweet grass in the field and the trough had just been filled with fresh water. He'd left enough grain for her for a day or so.

For some reason, he'd thought he needed to put out more grain. Now he understood the inspiration was a nudge. It was *Gott*'s way of helping him prepare for the journey he and Molly would need to take.

They continued walking until they arrived at an old woodshed still standing near a *haus* that had long been abandoned. The *haus* itself was all but falling apart. He would not feel safe bringing Molly in there. The floors might be rotten, and they'd tumble into the cellar.

He assisted her over some stacked-up wood and made a place for her to sit. Once she was seated, he built up a wall, blocking them in. It would look like a half-filled woodshed.

Satisfied he'd done everything he could do, Zeke joined Molly on their makeshift bench and prepared to wait out their would-be murderers. He was cold and stiff, but they had survived.

"Would you like my jacket?" he offered in a whisper.

She shook her head.

She was being the smart one, not speaking. He sighed. It might be a long wait.

Molly was relieved when Zeke ceased talking. He was a bold one, and she admired his brave spirit, but the situation called for a little more caution.

She had been touched by his offer to lend her his jacket. He had to be cold, too. The temperature had fallen dramatically since they'd first set out—was it only five hours ago?—to take care of Preacher Levi's horses. Since that time, they had been nearly run over, chased, forced to walk along a trail that resembled the edge of a ravine, got caught in a deluge, and now the killers had chased Zeke from his own home and business.

She was furious.

He, on the other hand, sat calmly as if a life of danger and excitement was the norm and not at all atypical for him. She wished she knew how he did it.

Finally, she couldn't stand it anymore. She leaned in close, doing her best not to be affected by the nearness. "How are you doing this? Acting so calm?"

He copied her actions, leaning in until she

felt the warmth of his breath on her lips. She licked her lip, then dropped her gaze, mortified.

He cleared his throat. His whisper had a husky edge she hadn't heard before. "I am not calm. Sitting here and not actively trying to solve this problem is one of the hardest things I have ever done in my life. Since I have no choice, I do the only thing I can do. I pray. I ask *Gott* to help me be still and to calm my racing mind."

She blinked. It had not occurred to her to pray.

"Does He hear you?" Should she have asked that? It showed him her vulnerability. Her weakness. She could not take the words back, though.

"*Ja.* He hears me. He hears you, too. He is our *Gut* Father, and He always hears us."

She wished she could believe that. "He let my *daed* and my fiancé die."

He nodded. "And my wife."

"Yet you still trust Him?" How? She wanted to comprehend his faith so badly she could taste it on the tip of her tongue.

"He will not take our freedom to choose

from us. We can choose Him, or we can choose the world. I chose Him."

Wow. It sounded so simple.

A car motor hummed closer. They both tensed, but did not leave their hiding place. Molly didn't know if it would do any *gut*, but she decided to put Zeke's beliefs into practice once again. Squeezing her eyelids tightly closed, she clasped her hands together on her lap and prayed. She didn't know if she used the correct words. Although, maybe it didn't matter what she said.

When she opened her eyes, she did not feel as though anything monumental had happened. She had not become a different person because she had opened her heart up to *Gott*. Or had she? It had not been noticeable at first, but some of the anxiety had fled her system. She knew they were still in danger. And there was a big chance that they would be injured or killed. At the same time, she had the feeling she was not alone in this anguish, and it was more than having Zeke at her side. So much more.

The vehicle driving past the *haus* moved agonizingly slow. A beam of light shot through the cracks between the wood stacked in front of them. She ducked lower, making sure her head remained below the wood line. For a moment, she did not completely get what they were doing, then she recalled something she had heard from the teenagers in the community. People liked to use bright spotting lights during deer season to find the fields where deer congregated. Well, deer season was months away, so she did not believe they were spotting for deer. They were using the lights to find them.

Had they seen them hiding in the woodpile? There truly was no place to go if they had. She and Zeke were blocked in by walls in back and on both sides, and a pile of wood in front of them, too high for her to jump over if they heard the men coming in their direction.

They waited, never moving a muscle. Molly developed an itch along the side of her nose, but she couldn't scratch it. She held her hands together, forcing herself to endure the pesky sensation. It was better than the alternative, which would mean she and Zeke would die.

Finally, the light dimmed. The engine revved and the car sped away.

"Did they give up?"

"Nee." He sounded too positive for her liking. "They'll keep searching. I think we are safe enough here for a few minutes."

She sighed and closed her eyes. She needed sleep. When she felt herself sagging, Zeke tugged her toward him and turned her so she was leaning against his shoulder.

"I'm okay," she mumbled. "We can walk."

His laughter made his body shake. Her head bounced against him. "Rest for a few hours. I'll wake you when it is time to go."

She yawned and relaxed against him, drifting into sleep.

She awakened to pitch-black. Her head leaned against the wall of the woodshed. Where was Zeke?

TEN

Zeke stood outside the woodshed, staring at the horizon. Molly wilted from relief. He was still here and he was safe. When she had awakened and not seen him, her mind conjured up a host of bad things that could have happened to him. Her relief changed, though, when she watched his posture. He was not a man viewing a relaxing sunrise. His rigid back told her more than words that he didn't like what he was seeing.

And that worried her a lot.

Zeke had been calm and unruffled most of the time she'd known him. For him to be concerned, she knew it had to a serious matter. Whenever he had become worried before, there had always been a *gut* reason. Molly had learned to trust his instincts these past two days.

Climbing around the wood piled in a wooden shield, she marched over to stand at his side. Following his gaze, she looked at the horizon. Colors were blooming on the lightening sky of a new day. As always, she was amazed at the beauty of it all. Something struck her as different, but she could not put her finger on it.

"What are we looking at?" she finally asked him.

"Well, on the bright side, the rain finally stopped around an hour ago."

"*Ja*, I noticed. Why do you not seem happy about that?" Not needing to duck between the drops seemed a *gut* thing in her mind.

"It took me a while to realize what I was seeing. I must be more tired than I thought. The colors are wrong."

Startled, she jerked her head up and took in the gorgeous array of hues again. This time she saw it. Her mouth fell open. The colors were still gorgeous, but looking at it now, she saw a hint of the ominous.

"I've never seen that green before in a sunrise."

His mouth firmed. "It's not supposed to be there. The only time I have ever seen that color in the sky before was when the weather conditions were right for a tornado."

That would be bad. How did one hide from a tornado without a basement or shelter? She'd heard of people being killed when hit by flying debris.

"Do we stay here, under the shelter?" She grimaced. The woodshed had been fine to protect them from the rain, but its suitableness for a tornado shelter was dubious.

"*Nee*. We must find better shelter. Preferably one that's not on raised ground. And we have to continue to keep watch for those men."

"What about the abandoned *haus*?" She pointed at the desolate-looking building.

He shook his head. "That won't hold. Look how the side wall is collapsing. Not to mention, it's probably home to all sorts of creatures, some of whom might bite."

She frowned. "I wish we had had time for me to look at the databases at the police station. If we had found either of the men who tried to kill me, you would at least know what they look like. As it stands, I am the only one of the two of us who knows. Doesn't that leave you vulnerable, though, too—to be with me?"

A crooked smile broke on his face. Unexpectedly, his hand touched her face and gently brushed back the hair that had come free from her braids.

"I'm not planning on getting far enough away from you that I might see them and you don't. I figure as long as we're together, you will see them and be able to warn me. Then, once the weather clears, we can go straight to the police station, and you can look at the databases."

She bit her lip. "Do you think the bishop will mind?"

He shrugged. "I doubt it. But by the time we get to the station, the chief will most likely have been in touch with your bishop. They will already be aware of what you can and cannot do."

He had a point.

As the sun continued to rise in the sky, the greenish cast became more evident. The clouds thickened and grew darker. They clumped together to form a wall that stretched across the sky as far she could see. There wasn't a hint of blue in the sky.

Her ears popped. She gasped and put her

hands over them, working her jaw to ease the pressure building against her eardrums.

"Molly! Are you all right? Are you in pain?" Zeke stood over her, his hands spread out as if he were ready to help her at any moment if only she would tell him what he needed to know.

"I'm okay," she assured him. "My ears suddenly popped. They did hurt, but only for a second. But I wasn't expecting it. It surprised me."

He nodded. "The air pressure changing. We will start walking. Let's keep close to the tree line when we can. When we are out in the open, we will have to be vigilant."

"If we were two teenagers on our *rumspringa*, we could dress in English clothes and blend in." She tossed him a grin.

He answered with a chuckle and a shake of his head. "If only. However, as two baptized adults, I do not think we can get away with that."

She agreed. She wasn't really serious, though. Even when she'd been a teenager, she'd had no interest in testing the boundaries.

They kept their talking to a minimum after

that. When a siren wailed in the distance, they both stopped and listened. The first, short wail was immediately followed by a longer one, one that held the same note for a full minute.

Eyes wide, her head whipped around to face Zeke. "They've seen one."

"*Ja*. A tornado has been spotted. It might be miles away, even in another county. That wail is warning us to take cover."

She whirled around, scouring the land for any possibilities. "Where? The land is completely flat and I don't see any *hauser*."

He glanced at her, his expression telling her he had no ideas. Suddenly, she grabbed on to his arms. "The bridge!"

There was a covered bridge a short distance from where they were. It was only one lane. While the bridge itself might not have been a safe hiding spot, they could hide against the embankment under it.

"*Ja!* It's our best hope. We can try to stay on the bank under it."

Reaching out, he grabbed hold of her hand and began to run. Her leg still ached, but she didn't dare slow down. They were attempting to outrun Mother Nature.

As if to mock them for their impudence, hail the size of golf balls began pelting them. Molly's prayer *kapp* was not meant to protect her from large icy projectiles. It was better than nothing. She reached down and hefted the hem of the rain slicker, holding it above her head. Within two minutes, the fields that had been green only minutes before were coated with large white balls.

It might have been pretty if they had not been out in the middle of it.

They kept running. The ground grew slick. They both slipped a couple of times. Molly almost fell clear to the ground. Zeke's strong arms pulled her upright a second before her nose hit the mud.

They couldn't take the time to regroup. They continued to run, knowing their lives depended on it.

Finally, they arrived at the bridge. It was completely empty.

Zeke assisted Molly to slide gently down the embankment to stand under the cover of the large red bridge. There were no windows in the structure, so no glass would fly if the winds blew too hard. They were below it, so hopefully, a tornado would neither be able to swoop them up nor throw dangerous debris on them.

It was the best shelter they could find, although it was still too out in the open for her. They were vulnerable to anything coming their way, whether it was killers or the weather.

"Get lower," Zeke told Molly. "We need to protect our heads if a tornado actually lands."

She swallowed loudly.

He wanted to tell her it would be all right. But no one could make such a promise. If he said that and things turned out badly, it would have been an unintentional lie.

He would never lie to her. Even if a lie would bring her comfort. Comfort based on fabrication did not last. The truth would always find its way into the light.

They crouched together against the rocks framing a small stream. He and his brothers used to *cumme* and fish here. They stood on the edge of the bank, inches from the water. He hoped they could remain dry here. Her feet had already been drenched once. Granted, these boots were better than the tattered ones she had been wearing. And her socks! He had been shocked at how thread-bare they were.

Next to him, she shivered. He moved closer, tucking her closer to keep her warm. She didn't protest, but snuggled into his side.

He glanced down at her *kapp*. It had been clean when he met her. Yet it clearly showed signs of age. Many young women her age would have bought or made a new one by now. But she hadn't. He recalled the younger girls. Their *kapps* and aprons had been fresher than hers had been.

Molly and Abigail had been supporting the family, he recalled her saying. She had been cleaning *hauser*. How well did that pay? He doubted it was enough. She had four others to feed. And she had a *haus* to care for. Not to mention upkeep on the land, keeping the horse fed.

Did she go without so her sisters could have better necessities? It seemed likely. Molly took her responsibilities seriously. He had no doubt she put herself last on the list when it came to providing what was needed.

Almost like a mother.

He frowned. Yesterday, when he had com-mented he'd name a daughter Daisy if he ever had one, she'd reacted as it his comment had hurt. But why? A young woman like her should want a family of her own.

Unless…

Unless the idea of courting and marrying a man other than Aaron was too painful for her. But he had seen signs that said she might have felt a glimmer of interest for him. Of course, such signs were quickly cut off.

So maybe she would not allow herself to think of marriage.

Was it Aaron? Or did it have to do with her injuries? He rubbed his chin on her *kapp*. Trying to figure her out was enough to give a man a headache.

The wind picked up. It blew cold and sharp against their faces. Molly let out a whimper. He wrapped his arms around her and held tight. He would hold her until the danger or her fear left.

Lifting her head, she gazed to the left. A soft gasp escaped her lips. He twisted to look at what she'd seen.

The rolling clouds roiled and writhed like a nest of vipers. Below the heavy clouds, a dark wall cloud descended. His stomach bottomed out. It spanned the entire visible horizon from where they stood. A single twisting rope fell from the massive clouds. Fascinated, he stared. The strand grew wider, twisting and spinning in an uneven, staggering path over the terrain.

And the noise! He'd heard a freight train a few times in his life. The tornado sounded like three trains running past at the same time. It devoured whatever got in its path without mercy.

A large tree was in its way. It must have stood in that spot for close to a hundred years. It did not matter. One moment the tree was there; the next it was sucked into the hungry tornado. A few yards later, the twister spit out the remains of the tree. Branches fell everywhere. They watched the tornado work its way across the field, sometimes touching the land, sometimes bouncing upward and spinning in the air.

They could feel the pull of the wind. It whipped at their clothes.

Molly shrank away, plastering herself against the wall, covering her head and neck with her hands. He moved in, desperate to shield her from the tornado.

It sailed over the bridge. For a moment,

he thought they were spared. Suddenly, the twister shot back down and slammed into the end of the wooden structure. Beams fractured and fell to the water below. A board about two by four feet slapped his leg on its way by. He would have a bruise for sure.

They pressed themselves closer to the rock and avoided the debris the best they could.

Just as quickly as it had started, the tornado disappeared. The sky remained ominous.

"You know," Zeke commented, keeping his voice casual, "I always thought I would like to see a tornado up close. I think I would like to revise that opinion now."

Seeing it appear had been awesome and amazing. But he had been filled with the need to protect Molly the entire time. Regardless of the awesomeness, he hoped to never repeat the experience. It wasn't worth the cost.

ELEVEN

Molly stared at him, incredulous. Her glance bounced to the destruction the twister had left in its path. She had never heard anyone say anything so bizarre. Who wanted to see a tornado? "Really? You've wanted to see a tornado up close? Why?"

It was the most irrational thing she had ever heard the very rational Zeke utter.

"I always wondered what they would sound like, or how a tornado would move across the ground. Now I know." She could hear the shrug in his voice.

She shook her head. "I suppose so. All I need to know is they are dangerous. Now what do we do?"

"I'm not sure." He glanced around, his gaze skimming over their surroundings. "The sky is getting lighter, which is a good sign. We haven't heard the sirens go off, so I don't know if it means there will be more or if we are safe to move on. Usually, there's a second siren to let us know the emergency is over."

He had a cousin who was a volunteer firefighter. He had learned lots of interesting details over the years. He had almost joined the department once when he was younger, but it was more difficult when you had a full schedule of clients to care for.

She pursed her lips and blew out her breath. "I do not want to sound like I doubt you, but I don't think this is as safe as we thought it was. Maybe we should keep looking for another place to shelter."

He glanced around, his narrowed gaze landing on the damaged bridge. Another stiff breeze would send more of the debris falling into the water. If it blew too hard, it could hit them where they stood.

"You could be right." He looked at the embankment, his face filled with doubt.

She knew what he was thinking. Climbing out of there would take a while. Plus, at least here they were still below the majority of the land. If a tornado did touch down again, the higher ground would be the most dangerous place to be. After a quick discussion, they decided to remain alongside the stream for the time being.

Molly was concerned about how they would climb out when they needed to. "The area next to the creek is so much more slippery."

"It might be a problem," Zeke told her. "I won't lie. But I think we will be able to find a spot where we can climb out. This isn't the only fishing area along the creek."

She bit her lip, pondering his words. Finally, she nodded her agreement.

Eventually, they set out at a steady pace, keeping their conversation to a minimum, always listening and watching for signs of pursuit or any more tornadoes touching down. At one point, the edge along the creek became too narrow to walk on and they had to either climb to higher ground or walk in the creek.

Zeke went first, sure he could pull Molly up if she had trouble. Unfortunately, the recent rain and storm had washed away some of the grit that normally provided traction. By the time they arrived at the top, they were covered with mud and grass. They weren't fit to be seen.

Molly swayed at first as she stood with

both feet on the wet ground. She was exhausted, achy and felt decidedly lopsided.

"Do you need help?" Zeke whispered.

"*Nee.* I will be fine. I think I broke one of the heels off your sister's boots." They had been such pretty boots, too. Molly didn't know Joss. She hoped the woman was kind and wouldn't be mad at Zeke for loaning them to her. "Will you get in trouble for letting me use them?"

He shrugged, unconcerned. "Joss isn't materialistic. She left them at my *haus* months ago and never came to retrieve them. I'm not worried about it. I am worried about you trying to walk with a broken heel. Is it your injured leg?"

She froze, then flushed. Of course, he would know one of her legs was injured. She limped. And she might have even mentioned it. It just was not something she liked to focus on. And having someone else mention it was enough to make her cringe with self-consciousness.

She shook herself out of it. He had lost family, too. One injured leg obviously didn't disturb him. She would not let it disturb her.

"It is. I don't know what I can do about it. I

have to wear shoes. And it would be painful to wear them on the wrong feet. Besides, the heel is not broken all the way off. I still have enough to walk on if I'm careful."

The glance he sent her reeked of skepticism. To his credit, he did not say anything. He continued walking. After a few steps, he said, "If you need help, will you ask for it?"

She grimaced. He had gotten to know her pretty well. "*Ja.* I will ask. If I need help."

Hopefully, she would not require his assistance. After ten minutes, he slowed and motioned for her to stop. She crossed her arms across her body, listening for what had made him stop.

Voices. He had heard people talking. After a few seconds, she was able to pick out what the two men were saying.

"She probably won't be any trouble, Scott. I'm tired. Had you noticed there was a tornado? Let's go home. We can look for her later."

"Are you serious? You're going to let some Amish chick get the better of you? I shot two people in front of her. I can't take that risk. She needs to be taken out of the picture. And you see who she's hanging out with. Cops and marshals. I don't know what her connection is with them, but she's a threat to everything we've worked for."

The other man laughed. "I killed cops for this job and am still waiting to get paid. I'm not doing any more until I get my share."

Her blood became icy sludge in her veins. They were calmly discussing murder. Hers and those they had already killed. Her eyes met Zeke's and widened. They blazed with anger in his taut face. She had never seen an Amish man so angry before.

"Cumme," she mouthed. Then she pointed in the opposite direction.

He visibly fought with his anger for a moment before giving in and heading away from the men. They had gone a few feet when one of the men—the one who had shot the police officers—said, "Say, do you hear something?"

They could not hang around and be found. Any moment, they would come crashing through the trees and find Molly and Zeke standing there, almost like they had been surrendering. Well, she had no intention of surrendering or dying today.

They continued walking, stepping in a

quicker pace, hiding behind the shrubs and trees when they could.

As she had expected, within a minute, the two killers came hunting for what had made the sound, thrashing around like a couple of bears. They had obviously never hunted or learned how to be still and unnoticed.

She and Zeke crouched down behind the densest bushes and brambles they could reach, staying close to the ground. Their black rain slickers helped to camouflage the colors of her rosy dress and his blue button-down shirt.

Two men stumbled into the clearing and stood less than five feet from where they hid. They had scowls on their faces and guns in their hands. The younger man also had a knife attached to his belt. It looked identical to the one sitting in the police station's evidence room. The one left quivering in her wall after he had thrown it at her.

No doubt it was the one he'd stabbed Parker with.

The other man huffed and puffed as he stood there.

"I can't hear anything with you breathing so hard."

"Can't…help…it. COPD."

Molly had no idea what COPD meant, but he obviously was not in *gut* health.

A duck quacking jarred her out of her thoughts. Where was the duck?

The younger man reached for his phone. He looked at the number and made a face. "Yes?… No, we don't have her yet. We're closing in on them. She's hanging out with some Amish dude. Maybe a boyfriend. Will we get paid extra if we take him out, too?"

Molly clutched at Zeke's hand.

The man held the phone away from his ear, a snarl twisting his face. The sound of a third man raging came through the device. Not well enough that she would be able to recognize the voice. But she knew it was a male voice. Unless the caller was using some sort of technology to disguise his voice. "All right. All right. I was just checking. We'll leave him alive, if we can."

The man called Scott listened to a few more instructions, then hung up. "Yeah, there's no way I'm leaving him alive."

"But you told the boss—"

"I know what I told him. But this guy's probably the reason we haven't caught her or gotten our money yet. I'll tell you what, Jeff, I'm not feeling very generous toward him."

After a few more grumbled comments, they stomped off, still searching. Molly and Zeke remained where they were for a bit to give them time to leave the area. Stunned at what she heard, Molly realized she was still holding Zeke's hand. She couldn't make herself release it. These men were set to kill her and Zeke. Suddenly she whipped her head toward him.

"There's a third man."

He nodded. "The one who hired them."

Zeke was torn between feeling sick to his stomach and so angry he could barely control it. Someone had hired two killers to go after sweet Molly. Who would do such a thing? The midmorning heat didn't help. He removed his rain slicker and held it over his arm. It was *gut* that Molly had pulled him away when she did. He'd never been so close to losing his temper. It would have resulted in their deaths.

"At least we have names for the men," he said, trying to inject some hope into his voice.

It was hard to feel hopeful, though, when you knew what you were up against.

"I hope that helps them find them." She cast her eyes around, looking uneasy. "I am not a vengeful person, but they need to be locked in a jail cell. For the rest of their lives, if possible. They would kill us and my family without batting an eye, ain't so?"

He sighed, then nodded. "I have to agree with you. It's a bit chilling to stand so close to someone who wants you dead. And for no other reason than that you were in the way and annoyed him. I annoy people all the time. Ask my brothers."

"What if we had to sneeze?"

He blinked. That was random. "Had you needed to sneeze while we were hiding?"

"*Nee*. Not this time. Stop grinning at me. I am serious. When I feel anxious, sometimes I sneeze. And not usually once. I sneeze four or five times in a row."

"That would not have been *gut*." They would never have made it out alive if she'd sneezed. "I'm glad you didn't have to sneeze."

They began walking, their steps brisk as they could make them with her broken heel as they fled away from their would be killers.

"We have to make it to a phone and call Micah," Zeke said. "He'll know what to do."

They kept all conversation to a minimum, only speaking when necessary, usually in one- or two-word utterances. Forty-five minutes later, they stood staring at a residential area. Phone and power poles were snapped in half as if they had been twigs. Splintered branches littered the yards and street. Power lines lay across *hauser* and cars, snapping and buzzing. At least one *haus* smoldered, its residents standing outside in their pajamas, tears running down their shocked faces. What a horrible way to lose your home.

They walked past the distraught family and their neighbors.

"That leaves the phones out of commission," she said, distress tightening her eyes.

"Don't worry. Landlines may be out. Cell phones should still work."

She furrowed her brow. "*Nee.* Not all of them. I think it depends what carrier you have. Didn't you hear the neighbor? The storm has messed with some of the cell signals."

He sighed. He had no idea what carrier Micah had. "Now what?"

"We have to find a place to stay until the phones are back on."

They turned the corner. Molly stumbled to a halt, her face bloodless.

The older man, the one who had shot the officers, stood before them, a gun in his hand. He smiled, a nasty grin. "Well, Scott chose to look in the wrong place. Looks like I'm going to be the one to finish the job."

Not if Zeke could help it. Grabbing his rain slicker, he tossed it over the man's unsuspecting head.

"Run!" he yelled to Molly.

He'd keep her safe no matter what.

TWELVE

Zeke pushed Molly into a run, falling in behind her. The man yelled and swore, his voice muffled by the slicker. Within a few seconds, though, his shouting came through crystal clear. He'd gotten free. Which meant any moment, he'd begin shooting.

Directly ahead, a group of residents were congregated in front of a couple of *hauser* that had sustained substantial damage. Making a snap decision, Zeke grabbed her hand and pulled her away from them. He wouldn't be responsible for other people getting shot or killed. The man pounded after them. A gun barked. The shot went wild, lodging into the side of a *haus*. People screamed. They kept running.

A second yell. The younger man had joined the chase.

Zeke grew desperate. The older man they'd outrun with no problem. The second one? He was young, fit and determined. With the heel on Molly's boot broken, they would never make it.

Unless he bought her some time.

"Molly." She didn't look at him. She kept running. He heard her breathing hard. She probably couldn't answer. How long would she last against the two of them? His determination hardened like steel. "Listen. Keep running. No matter what you hear. Don't stop."

"Wait!" she grabbed his arm, her hand like a vise. "You're not leaving me. Don't. You. Dare."

They dashed behind a large van. He peered out. The two men weren't on to them. Not yet. They were looking, though.

"Molly, we have no other choice. They'll kill you."

She shook her head, her mouth in a stubborn line. "And if you give yourself up to them, they'll kill you. I'm not going to let that happen."

"Neither am I," a man's voice said.

He recognized that voice!

They both gasped and spun. Neil, his former driver, frowned at him. "You in trouble, Zeke?"

He remembered his doubts about the man. He'd wondered if Neil could be involved with something evil. But Neil hadn't been with them. And he didn't think he was the man on the phone, either. He'd heard the tone in the voice enough to know it was no match for Neil's.

He went with his instincts.

"*Ja*. We're in trouble. Two men are out to kill us."

Neil's jaw dropped open. "Are you kidding me? Why would someone want to kill you?" When neither of them changed the story, he rubbed the back of his head. "You'll have to explain it to me later, but I'll help you any way I can."

Zeke paused for a moment before deciding to trust Neil. "Is your van nearby?"

Neil patted the van they were hiding behind with pride. "This is it. I traded in my old one yesterday."

"Can you drive us out of here?" They might both survive this nightmare.

"Sure. Where do you need to go?"

Zeke glanced at Molly. The anger had dissipated, leaving hope in its wake. "We really need to go to the police station."

Neil shrugged. "I can do that for an old friend. Think of it as an apology for being a jerk yesterday."

"No apology needed. We are old friends, after all, ain't so?" He may even reconsider hiring Neil again once this was all over.

Neil opened the sliding side door of the van. "Hurry up and get in. Keep low. I don't need my tires shot out."

Molly and Zeke popped into the van and crouched into the back seats. Neil closed the door, then sauntered around to the front, trying to act casual. Zeke smiled grimly. Acting wasn't his strength. But he had a *gut* heart, despite Zeke's earlier concern.

It didn't take long to get to the station, but once there, Zeke wasn't sure they'd reached safety.

"Looks like the lights are out here, too." Neil parked in the side lot. Although cars were there indicating the police were working, the windows were dark, as was the lobby.

"Will they let us in?" Molly asked, trepidation in her voice. If they didn't, they'd be out of options. Where else could they go to escape the men coming for them?

"Look, how about this?" Neil twisted around in his seat. "I will go in and see if there is someone who will speak to me. I will tell them that Zeke and—" He lifted a brow at Molly.

"Molly," she supplied.

"Great. I will tell them I have Zeke and Molly in my van. Is there anyone I should ask for?"

"My brother-in-law, Sergeant Steve Beck, or my brother, Deputy Marshal Micah Bender. Either of them will work."

Neil's eyebrows climbed high on his forehead. "I never realized you had ties to the police. And the marshals. Whoa. Seriously cool."

His ears grew warm. He had not meant to sound like he was bragging about his family. "I wanted to make sure they knew who was out here. My brother knows our situation. He will know what to do if he's here."

He hoped. He had no idea how serious a complication it would be having the phones and electric down. Micah probably felt like he was living Amish again. The thought amused him for a brief moment.

"Okey dokey. You kids stay hidden. I don't want anything happening to my pretty new van." They watched out the front window as his figure grew smaller. He disappeared into the building.

"Do you think they'll be able to help us?" Molly asked, her voice hushed.

"I do. They are both used to handling crisis circumstances. I'd say this qualifies."

She nodded, her head drooping against his shoulder. He smiled down at her. She had been through a lot. But she had not given up. Nor had she ever indicated she was uncomfortable. She had to have been, several times. Between her leg and the drenching she got yesterday it had not been a picnic. Yet he knew if he said they needed to leave the van and find a different hiding spot, she'd go along with it. She might argue, but if his reasoning was sound, she'd agree.

That kind of trust was priceless.

Without thinking, he bent to kiss the top of her head. At the same time, she lifted her head and looked at him. The kiss landed squarely on her cheek.

They froze, staring at each other. "Why did you kiss me?"

Heat flooded his neck all the way to his forehead. Somehow, he didn't think *because I wanted to* was the correct response.

But he had wanted to for a while. Kissing was not something an Amish man did lightly. He had not courted her or walked her home from church. He was not a young man anymore. He'd be thirty-two on his next birthday. Eight years' difference lay between them.

But did it matter?

"I had not planned on kissing you. It was spontaneous. And actually, I was aiming for the top of your head."

"That doesn't really answer my question."

He knew it didn't. But it was the only answer he had for her. He was still in shock that he had tried to kiss her, even on the head. That was not the kind of thing he did. He was not spontaneous. Except with Molly.

Glancing up, relief hit him. Micah and Neil were returning. Neil threw open the door and Micah poked his head in. When he caught sight of Zeke's red face and Molly's rosy cheeks, he gave Zeke a brotherly *What are you doing?* kind of look.

Micah reached back and helped Molly hop out of the vehicle, leaving Zeke to fend for himself. He could not tell if Molly was mad at him or confused. When she turned her head and offered him a shy smile, he grinned.

Things were getting interesting.

He had kissed her. Sort of. Molly flushed again as she strode into the precinct at Micah's side. She had only been kissed a couple of times before and that wasn't until after she and Aaron were engaged.

Inside, it wasn't as dark as she'd expected. "I thought the electricity was off?"

Micah opened a door and gestured for them to enter. "It is. The landline phones are out, too. Places like the police station, the fire station and the hospital have backup generators in case something like this happens. It's important to keep the life-saving services up and running in an emergency."

She thanked him for explaining it. She had lived her whole life with limited exposure to such things until the accident. Then she was overwhelmed by them. Ambulances, hospitals, physical therapy. She'd experienced them all. The only thing she didn't experience was the coroner and the funeral services. Amish didn't use funeral homes. Her *daed* and Aaron had been buried in a simple Amish funeral. She was still in the hospital when their services were held. So was her *mamm*.

Micah led them into a small conference room similar to the one she'd been in the other day. "We talked with your bishop. He has allowed us to use the database with you only as long as the men who attacked you are unidentified. If you identify both, we'll shut down the process immediately."

"Of course. I have no interest in looking at it for any other reason."

The door opened, and several other officers entered the room. Including the chief and Steve.

"Before we have you begin, we need to know what happened at the safe house."

She paled. She had not forgotten about the officers who had died for her. It was clear from their grim, unsmiling faces that these officers were aware of their deaths. They needed her to tell them how it happened. Her gut twisted at the memory. She clutched at her stomach as if she could hold it still.

"It was awful. Those poor men."

Zeke scooted his chair closer to her until they were nearly touching. His warmth settled her enough so she could keep going.

"Start at the beginning, please." Micah's words were dispassionate, but his tone was not. He was torn up about it, she realized. They all were. These men were their colleagues. Their friends.

"When I got to the safe *haus*, I was so tired. I went to my room and fell right to sleep. I did not even take the time to dress for bed or take off my boots. I didn't even get their names. I regret that." She swallowed, the grief of the moment sweeping over her. "Early the next morning, the police officer who drove me the night before woke me up very abruptly. He said we had to leave."

She told them about seeing the dead officers in the living room. They all winced. Steve had tears in his eyes. She looked away while he wiped them on his sleeve, giving him as much privacy as she could. Next, she related going to the pole barn and taking that vehicle. "I thought we were safe, until the other car chased us. It came up to us so fast."

She told how he'd disabled their car. "The officer gave me a compass he had in his glove compartment. He told me to follow it north until I saw things I recognized. Then he got out and began shooting the other car. I did what he said. I ran. The man in the other car came after me, but he wasn't able to catch me. I got a *gut* look at his face."

The chief nodded once. "That will help us find him. Please continue."

Keeping to the details, she told them about finding herself near Zeke's *haus* and going to him for help. When she got to the part about going with him to Preacher Levi's, Zeke took up the narrative. She listened as his soothing voice related the destruction of his farrier wagon. Micah winced at that, but Zeke kept telling the story. When he mentioned the men invading his home, Micah and Steve sat up. She shivered. Zeke reached out and took her hand but didn't glance her way. His brother had noticed.

They related the tale about surviving the tornado by hiding under the bridge, and the conversation they'd overheard, including the names of the criminals. Micah literally growled. "He wants to kill my brother because he can?"

"We will get him, Micah." Chief Spencer

glanced around the room, his face cold. "We will get them both and we will discover who hired them."

To the man, the other officers all nodded, united in their grief for their fallen friends.

Chief Spencer addressed her directly. "Molly, we want to thank you for coming in today. We know it's been a rough couple of days for you and Zeke. It is our hope that what you do today will lead us to these men."

"Yes, sir. I hope so, too." How would she ever sleep at night knowing they were out there, hunting for her?

She was tired of being a victim. Today, she would begin taking her life back.

THIRTEEN

Molly was led to another room and told to make herself comfortable in front of a computer screen. The receptionist brought her and Zeke bottled waters and showed them where the restrooms were. She had a brief feeling of déjà vu, but shoved the thoughts away, refusing to dwell on the last time she departed from this police station and the catastrophic events that followed.

"Take your time and look at the pictures carefully. Some of the images are old, or the person may have changed the way they wear their hair, added a beard. Try to remember the person you saw and see if his eyes, the shape of his nose, all the little details, match up."

Molly pressed her lips together. She would do her best, but she had only seen him for a few moments. What if she missed him and he went free? If she didn't find him, she'd always wonder if it was because she didn't pay enough attention to the small details.

She sat in front of the computer database, her belly doing flip-flops inside her. Would she find one or both of them? And if she did, would it lead to the discovery of the boss? The man who had paid them to kill innocent people. Zeke grabbed a chair and pulled it alongside hers.

"I've seen these guys now, too," he reminded her. "If we both look, maybe we'll find them sooner."

Some of the tension left her. Zeke had an eye for the smaller details.

"Maybe. If they're here." She stared at the screen. "I'm not even sure how to work this."

"*Ach.* Neither am I. It can't be that hard, ain't so?" Zeke looked at it again, then got up and left the room.

So much for it not being that difficult. At least she was not the only one flummoxed by the technology.

A moment later, he returned with the receptionist.

"I am sorry," she said and smiled. "I thought you had been shown how to use this."

She patiently demonstrated how to move from one page to the next and what to do when they found the criminals they were searching for. "If you need any additional help, don't hesitate to ask. That's what I'm here for."

They thanked her and watched as she walked out on needle-thin high heels. Molly could never understand how women walked in shoes like that. The low heels on Joss's boots had been difficult enough. Shaking the ridiculous thought from her brain, she turned her attention to the daunting task in front of her and drew in a deep breath to prepare herself. Zeke's presence steadied her.

Saying a quick prayer, she began.

It was overwhelming. The sheer volume of men and women in the database stunned her. Some of them were so young, she couldn't stem the sadness welling up. Zeke's hand latched onto hers again. He always seemed to know when she needed comfort.

"It's okay, Molly. I am here to help you though this."

"Oh, Zeke. It's awful. He's so young. Some are younger." Her voice cracked.

He squeezed her fingers. "I know. And

you're right. It is sad. But we have a job to do right now."

She nodded. She had to do this. Those officers were counting on her, even if they didn't know it. Nancy Stevens needed her to help her find justice. Thankfully, Terry had survived his wounds and was in the hospital—Micah had told them shortly after they'd arrived. The doctors were keeping him in a medicated sleep to help his body heal, so the police had not questioned him yet. When he was ready, they would release him from the comatose state he was in and he'd be able to resume his own life. How she wished it were that simple with Caleb.

Although, what kind of life would it be? His mother was gone forever. He had obviously known Scott before. She had to wonder if his association with the man had somehow led to Nancy's demise.

She switched gears before the topic could bring her down.

They searched for over an hour. There had to be an easier way. However, growing up Amish, this kind of technology wasn't something they used on a daily basis. Besides, it would be awful to miss something important because they took a short cut. They were both on their second water bottle before they finally found something relevant. At the top of the page, a young man's hard face stared out at her. Molly almost missed him. The picture on the database was old. He'd been so young, but it was clearly the man who had shot both Nancy and Terry. It was terrifying, looking at his cold face and eyes, knowing that young man was a cold-blooded killer.

"That's him." She pointed the picture out to Zeke. He scrutinized it the way she had.

"You're right. It was hard to tell at first, but now, looking at it, I can see the resemblance. His hair is different and he has some facial hair, but it's him."

"Let's look for his partner in crime. I heard him call him Jeff." She continued to scroll through the images. One by one, they examined them closely. Then they went back to the beginning. Jeff wasn't in the database. While she was happy they found the first killer, she was sad they didn't find the second.

"They'll have to find him another way, but we know Scott has been located. Now all the police have to do is find where he is physically and pick him up." He nudged her with his shoulder. "I have heard from my brother and Steve that sometimes when one criminal is arrested, he will give up his partner, either so he doesn't get away with it or in the hopes that the sentence will be lighter."

She sighed. "I don't want them to get light sentences. They killed people."

He rubbed her hand. "We're closer than we were. I think having a name to put with the face is huge progress."

When the chief came in, he agreed with Zeke. "You have helped us tremendously. We didn't have any leads before this, and now we have this."

"You're right. I was hoping to get them all today."

Zeke looked puzzled. "You have no leads? What about the husband? I have listened to my brother enough to know the spouse is always a suspect until they can prove their innocence."

Molly stared at him, aghast. "The spouse?"

She couldn't comprehend marrying someone and later being able to do harm to them.

The chief grimaced, giving an apologetic kind of shrug. "I forgot that you had not heard the latest news. It's not good, I'm afraid. It seems sometime last night, Frank Stevens was murdered and his body was left in his car before the vehicle was set on fire."

Her stomach lurched. Zeke leaped past her and grabbed a garbage can. He was just in time. She vomited into the can, losing what little food she'd had. Afterward, the kind receptionist helped her into the restroom to clean up. She was too tired to even feel embarrassed at reacting so violently.

All she could think of was Terry Stevens. She had never liked the young man. He'd been arrogant, rude at times, and had looked down on her. She had tried to avoid him when she could. Then he had risked his life to save her. She would never forget that.

Until today, he had at least one parent. Now, he had no one. She recalled Nancy saying once that both she and Frank were only *kinder*, and their parents had all passed away.

Terry was alone in the world.

When she got herself under control, she returned to the office. Zeke was there alone.

She raised her eyebrows. "Where is everyone?"

"The chief wanted to give you a few minutes to collect yourself. He felt bad about telling you this way."

Her eyes welled up. She hated to cry, yet it was all she ever seemed to do these days. "I know you said *Gott* won't abandon us, and He is always with us. We believe in Him and trying to do what is right. But what about people like Terry? I never got the impression that Nancy or Frank had any sort of relationship with *Gott*. And Terry certainly never gave me the feeling that he believed either. Now he's in a hospital in a coma. When he wakes up, no one will be there to greet him or give him a hug. He'll be alone, and there is nothing to be done about it."

She didn't mean to sound so angry. Her whole body felt bruised and her spirit was searching for answers.

Zeke edged in closer to her. When he touched her shoulder, she didn't think. Turning to face him, she threw herself into his arms. When they closed in around her, comforting her, she felt herself shatter. She wept on his shoulder, sobbing out her sorrow for Terry and his parents, for the officers who had given the lives for her, for the losses her own family had suffered and for herself.

She wept until she had no more tears to cry. And then she rested, feeling His presence as she surrendered and allowed Him to use Zeke to minister to her.

Zeke held on to Molly while she wept. Part of it was grief, he knew. She'd seen so much death and pain in the past few days. He murmured words of comfort to her bent head, without paying attention to what he was saying. All his concentration centered on the woman nestled securely in his arms as if she were meant to be there.

His heart ached with her. He knew how it felt to question *Gott*. He'd done it, too, after Iris died. His *daed* had not reprimanded him for his anger. Instead, his *daed* had counseled him to bring his anger directly to *Gott*. What had started as an angry conversation had given way to a talk between a wounded *kind* and his loving Father.

If only he could show that to others!

When Molly's tears stopped, he waited. She didn't pull out of his arms, as he had expected she would. *Nee*, she remained, snuggled close to his heart, resting. Every once in a while, she would sniff or shift slightly.

Contentment filled him. He would stay like this until she moved away. He would give her what she needed without demanding more or rebuffing her.

They stood that way for five minutes before she began to make movements indicating she wanted him to release her. Immediately, he let her go. His arms fell to his sides. They felt bereft without her tucked in them, but it wasn't about what he wanted. This was about Molly and what she needed to feel whole.

She let out a long, calming breath, then raised her glance to meet his.

He forestalled the words he knew were coming. "Please do not apologize. I understand. You have been so strong, Molly. I'm glad I was here for you when you needed it."

"I feel more at peace now. I have to disagree, though." Her mouth twisted into a self-deprecating smile. "I don't know how you can say I've been strong. I've cried more these past three days than I have in the past two years."

He shrugged. "Maybe that's part of it. If you didn't let yourself grieve then, you needed to at some point."

A discreet knock on the door halted whatever comment she had opened her mouth to make. The chief poked his head in. "Sorry to disturb you. We would like to talk with you if you feel up to it?"

Zeke and Molly followed the chief back to the main conference room. It was brimming with law enforcement. Molly moved closer to his side. He did not think she was aware of it, but his pulse skipped when her arm brushed against his own.

The chief indicated the two chairs at the front of the room. They walked over and sat in them. Steve and Micah sat flanking them. Chief Spencer raised his arms for silence, and it spread in a wave through the room.

"Folks, I know we are all grieving right now, and I respect that. It is imperative, however, that we remain focused on our goal, which is to apprehend the killer, Scott Davis, his partner, who at this time is only known as 'Jeff,' and the man who hired them both to kill our officers, Molly Schultz and possibly Zeke Bender." A murmur began at that. "And I suspect Nancy and Frank Stevens were also contract kills."

"Sir?" An officer in the back raised his hand.

"Yes, Michaels?"

"Sir, until the electric is reestablished, we have no phones. I suggest it would be easier to protect Miss Schultz if she remained here."

Molly's eyes widened.

Zeke frowned at Micah. Micah gave a single nod. "Officer Michaels is correct. No electricity does make it a challenge. Especially since law enforcement is stretched, coping with the damage in the city from the tornado that struck. I suggest that we return to Miss Schultz's home. We can have officers on duty there."

"You already tried that. Your partner was injured."

Zeke didn't see the woman who offered that suggestion, but he didn't need to. He was watching Molly's face. Therefore, when she raised her hand, he wasn't surprised.

"Yes, Molly." The chief acknowledged her.

"Um, I don't mean to interrupt. But would it make sense for me to join my family in Pennsylvania? Can't you have someone drive me there, and ask the Pennsylvania police to post guards or something? Then you can all stay here and keep searching for the men out to kill me."

The chief considered her words for a moment. "I suppose that would work, but, Molly, Pennsylvania is out of our jurisdiction."

"I volunteer to drive her," Steve said.

"I'll go along, too." Micah leaned back in his chair.

Zeke was stunned. She was leaving. Would he ever see her again?

The chief made a few additional comments before dismissing the officers. Zeke stood next to Molly. "I need to talk to you."

Micah caught his eye and walked away. He pulled Steve along. When it was only the two of them, Zeke looked her directly in the eyes.

"If you are going to Pennsylvania, I'm going with you."

She blinked. "But what about your work? Your family?"

"There's nothing that won't hold for a few days. I will not remain here wondering if you are okay or if Scott and Jeff came after you. I won't do it."

She stared at him, gauging his sincerity. Adrenaline pulsed through his veins. Would she let him *cumme* with her? He could not force her to bring him, nor would he want to. But he had been honest. Remaining behind would be agony, never knowing how she was or where she was. After an eternity, she nodded.

His shoulders slumped. He had not expected her to agree so quickly.

"I need to stop by my *haus* and collect a few items." She waved at her ensemble. "I can't go for any length of time wearing boots with a broken heel. I also want to check on my horse, make sure she's okay."

"I'll talk with Micah. He can find someone to care for the animals."

Steve and Micah were talking with the chief when they exited the room.

"Are you all set?" Steve raised his eyebrows.

"I need to collect some things at my *haus* first," Molly said.

"We can do that." Micah looked at his watch. "Let's get moving. I want to get you safe and settled. Zeke? What are your plans?"

Steve startled at that. Zeke tightened his jaw, daring his brother-in-law to tease him. "I'm Pennsylvania bound. With Molly."

Micah smirked. "I thought so."

As they headed out to the car, he heard Steve mutter to Micah, "You were right. I totally missed that one."

Micah chuckled. "You need to be more observant."

Zeke decided he didn't want to know.

Was she doing the right thing? Molly debated in her mind the choices she had as they made their way to Micah's car, but it always came down to the fact that she couldn't go anywhere with someone being in danger. If she remained at her *haus*, the police would have to watch her and take care of the town. If she remained at the precinct, officers who should be helping people would have to stay behind and babysit her.

At least in Pennsylvania, there would be more officers to protect them. She could blend in with the large Amish community there. At home, they were in a more remote area. And the killers didn't seem to know about her family in Pennsylvania.

And Zeke would be with her.

Her pulse kicked up a notch at the thought. She had not planned on having him *cumme*. She should have told him to remain with his family. That was where he belonged. But when he'd looked at her so tenderly, she had caved.

He felt something for her. As incredible

as it seemed, they appeared to have formed a connection over the past three days. It was fast. Too fast. She didn't trust it to last. Once the danger was done, she figured all the intense emotions would drain away.

She would miss him. Terribly. But for the moment, he was here. And he was becoming a solid support through the trials. She could not have made it this far without him at her side. How hard would it be to learn to go back to life without him once this was all done? She was not ready to think about that yet.

They settled into the back of Micah's vehicle.

"How long do you think you'll need to get ready?" Steve glanced back from the front passenger seat and made eye contact with her. "I told my wife things might be a little hectic for the next few days. She knows to go and stay with her parents if she has to."

Guilt seared her again. Because of her, Steve and his wife were separated.

"I keep telling you not to go there." Zeke frowned at her, obviously picking up on her sadness. "It's not your fault that Steve is not with my sister right now. This is Steve's job. It's the job he chose, the job he loves. So, if it wasn't you, he would be doing something else very similar right now."

"Zeke is correct. None of this is your fault and no one blames you for anything. The only person responsible is the one who pulled the trigger."

"Fine. To answer your question, I'm fairly certain I can get my things together in under fifteen minutes. I will not need to bring much with me. My cousin Susie is about my size, so I can borrow clothes from her if I need to."

"We will be at your house in about five minutes. When we stop, I want you to stay in the car and wait until Steve and I give you the go-ahead." Micah glanced back at her from the rearview mirror. "I'm sorry if I am being bossy."

Molly shook her head. "I am alive because of you and people like you. I'm not worried about if you are bossy with me."

The moment the SUV swung into her driveway, Molly's body tensed like a bow pulled taut. She reached out to Zeke. He met her halfway, catching her hand and holding tight. They didn't look at each other. Both of them watched Micah and Steve walk the perimeter and check the inside of the *haus*.

Finally, Micah waved for them to *cumme*. Molly left the car and ran to the door of the *haus*, her broken heel making her gait awkward, but all she cared about was getting out of the open. She felt like there was a target on her back. She bounced on her toes inside the door until it closed behind Zeke.

Then she was able to relax.

She had promised Steve under fifteen minutes, and she had every intention of keeping that promise. She cleaned up and replaced the broken boots with a worn pair that, while not the most comfortable, were at least intact. Then she threw a few items into her bag and put on a fresh dress and *kapp*.

"I'm ready!" she sang as she lifted the bag and sailed out to the kitchen.

Scott Davis stood in the doorway, grinning. "Well, that was easy. All I had to do was walk in here and you came to get me."

Zeke darted into the room and placed himself between Molly and Scott.

The assassin lifted his shoulders in a shrug. "It doesn't matter who dies first. I was planning on killing you both anyway."

"Not today you won't," Micah growled behind him. "US marshal. Drop your weapon. I have a gun aimed directly at you."

"And I have your partner handcuffed in the car, singing like a bird." Steve walked into the room and gently nudged Molly and Zeke out of the way. "He says you've gone rogue. The boss canceled the contract this morning."

Scott scowled. "He owes me."

"It's over," Micah announced.

She saw it the moment he made his decision. Scott had no intention of surrendering. He preferred death to jail. He swung his gun wildly and clocked Steve on the side of the head. Dashing around the dazed policeman, he grabbed Molly out of Zeke's arms and placed the gun against her side. "We'll die together, sweetheart."

They all heard it. He was going to shoot. Just because he could. She would die.

Micah's bullet hit him as he pressed the gun into her side. He flew back. His finger continued to pull the trigger, shattering the kitchen window.

It was over.

FOURTEEN

It had only been three days, but it felt odd entering her home again. Especially since it looked like it did Tuesday evening. And smelled like it, too. She wrinkled her nose.

"*Ach*. The dinner Abigail cooked is still sitting on the stove." She walked over and lifted the lid of the pan. The overripe aroma billowed out of the dish and attacked her nostrils. She gagged and slammed it closed again. "That definitely needs to be thrown out."

"It didn't smell appetizing?" Zeke tossed her a grin. Micah rolled his eyes.

"Hardly. I will need to soak these before I can clean them."

Her eyes drifted around the room and came to rest on the spot Parker had lain, bleeding.

"Hey." Zeke tugged the strap on her *kapp*. "He will be well. In a few weeks, he will be able to return to full duty. That's what Micah told me."

"Truly?" She glanced between the two brothers.

Micah nodded and moved to stand in front of her. "Yes. Parker left the hospital this morning. At this very moment, he is at home, resting, and his mom and dad insisted on coming to visit him so she could mother him."

She quirked an eyebrow. "He doesn't look like one who enjoys being mothered."

Micah grinned. "Nope. He's not. But he adores his mom, so he won't do anything to hurt her feelings. I've met her. She knows this and completely takes advantage."

Her heart melted at the story of a tough deputy US marshal who was unwilling to upset his mother. "Thank you for telling me he will be fine. I have been wonderful worried about him."

"I'll let him know." He grinned. His grin faded and a serious expression flattened his face. His blue eyes, so like Zeke's, grew sad. "I should also tell you that the families of the officer and the deputy marshal killed while guarding you have been notified."

She leaned against the counter, her legs

suddenly weak. Then his words penetrated. "Officer? They weren't both killed?"

He shook his head. "Officer Wright, who drove you away from the scene, is critically injured. The doctors are hopeful."

She stared at him. "I saw his eyes. They were staring wide open."

"He was shocked and dazed. The killer shot him a second time, which was why he is in the hospital still. Otherwise, he may have walked away from the scene."

She shook her head, amazed. "I do not know how he was not killed, but I am wonderful glad he lived. He saved my life."

"His Kevlar vest saved his life," Micah responded. "Also, before I forget to tell you, your animals have been cared for while you gone."

"Oh! I am so relieved. Who cared for them?"

He shrugged. "I talked with Chief Spencer and we made sure it got done."

Gratitude welled inside her. She had been watched over even while she was on the run.

Zeke sat at the table, pondering all that had happened in the past few days. Poor Molly. She had been through so much. Still, she had finally been allowed to *cumme* home. The men who had been after her were either on their way to the morgue or prison. And soon they would find out who the boss was. When that happened, she could finally rest and have peace of mind.

It bothered him that the police had not caught the ringleader yet. They were searching for his identity, and he'd heard some speculation that the man had learned his hired killers had been found and he was on the run. He had asked Micah about it. While his brother did not directly answer, probably couldn't answer, he gained the impression that Micah believed the man to be still around, waiting for his chance to spring.

He had decided to sleep on Molly's couch until they did catch him. He wouldn't let down his guard until he knew for sure that Molly was safe and didn't need to worry about criminals coming after her anymore.

Micah's phone rang. He gestured to the door, then walked outside to take the call. Zeke watched his brother leave, his mind whirring. Micah, Isaiah and Zeke had all suffered irreparable damage due to Joss's abduction when she was a toddler. Micah and Zeke had healed. And his brother Gideon presented a smiling face to the world. He was something of a prankster. But Zeke knew he had a serious side. He'd learned to cope through his humor.

Zeke turned to watch Molly. When he had first met her again after so many years—was it less than a week ago?—she'd been friendly but reserved. He'd seen insecurity and aloofness wrapped around her like a cloak. Now, she had confidence. Her smile, when she beamed it his way, no longer had that guarded quality.

She had also grown in faith. He had seen it in her eyes when he talked about *Gott*. She didn't put emotional distance between them at the mention of anything spiritual.

Suddenly, he recalled the way his wife talked about *Gott*. Zeke had felt His presence in his life and had never doubted He was there. Even when tragedy struck. Iris didn't have that same perspective. In fact, she had viewed *Gott* as a distant power rather than a loving Father. Why had they gotten together? It seemed strange now that he would marry someone who had such fundamentally different beliefs.

In the end, maybe it wasn't Zeke she didn't trust. Iris didn't trust that *Gott* had hers, and Danny's, best interests at heart. She didn't believe He would save her brother because she didn't see Him as her Father.

His mind reeled at the revelation. For so long he had blamed himself for her death. But it had not been his fault. In fact, he couldn't have saved her because her issues were with *Gott* and not him. He had done all he could. He had loved her and honored her. The rest had been beyond his control.

Micah returned to the *haus*, tucking his phone away as he entered the room. Zeke saw his brother's flat expression and rose to his feet. "Something has happened."

It wasn't a question.

"Yeah. I have to go. The coroner is asking to see both Steve and me ASAP. I also checked my voice mail and there's a message from Steve. Apparently, Terry's awake and feeling talkative. He wants to talk with Molly."

"Why?" Zeke burst out. "She's been through enough."

"Easy, bruh. I agree. But I think this needs to be her decision. Steve said the guy seems genuine. He's not angry. Just very sad and depressed. His mother was killed."

Zeke listened as Micah retold the details

of his conversation with their brother-in-law. He still didn't care for the idea of her going to see the man, but Micah had a point. Zeke had no authority to make decisions for Molly.

"I'll talk to her," he promised his brother.

"Good. That's all you can do. Then support her no matter what she decides."

"*Ja*. I can do that." He considered what Micah had said about his other call. "You probably can't tell me about what the coroner says..."

Micah rolled his eyes and walked out. "If it's something that pertains to you or Molly, I'll consider it. It will be a need-to-know basis. If you don't need to know, I won't tell you."

"I can live with that." He stood on the front step until his brother had driven away. Then he went to find Molly. He followed the sounds of clinking dishes to the kitchen. She'd been hard at work while he'd been ruminating about the past and talking with his brother.

When he joined her at the sink, she tossed him a smile. He couldn't help himself. He reached out and brushed some soap off her cheek. When she flushed, he grinned at her.

"Where's Micah?"

He recalled his mission. "He had to leave.

The coroner wants to see him and Steve immediately."

Those blue eyes brightened. "About?"

"We think alike. I told my brother I wanted to know. He promised if we needed to know, he'll tell us."

She turned back to the sink and wiped her hands dry with the dish towel lying on the counter.

"Something else you need to know."

"Ja?" She raised her eyebrows at him.

"Micah said Terry Stevens is awake. He wants to talk with you."

Her mouth dropped open and she blanched. He led her to the table. She sat and stared at him. "Why would he want to talk with me?"

"I asked Micah the same thing. Micah said Terry had wept when he learned his mother was truly dead. He'd also been stunned to hear Scott Davis had apparently murdered his father."

His brother had also said with Scott dead, it would take some digging to uncover the truth. He knew his brother wouldn't give up until he'd learned all he could.

"I want to visit him," she decided. Then she paused, as if she was unsure of her next question. "Would you *cumme* with me?"

He nodded. "*Ja.* I will go with anywhere you need to go."

She blinked, her cheeks pink, at the declaration. "The hospital will do for now."

He kept his silence. Now wasn't the time to talk about the possibility of courting. They had too much trauma to sort through before they could return to their regular lives.

He would wait.

Still flustered, Molly climbed into her buggy. Without thinking about it, she shifted over and let him sit on the right, the spot reserved for the husband in Amish families. Her flush deepened.

"Do you want to drive or shall I?" he asked.

Trembling, she passed the reins to him. Her hands were quaking too much, she told herself. In her heart, though, she liked having him take that spot. If only...

She shut the thought down. He was helping her, protecting her. Soon, he'd return to his *haus*, and she'd have her family to tend. She refused to waste time dreaming for what could never be hers. Other women got married and had *kinder*. Not women with physical and emotional scars and burdened with so many responsibilities. To hold on to that dream would be selfish.

She'd let it go after she returned to her life. Today, she'd enjoy Zeke's strong presence for as long as she had him at her side.

At the hospital, Zeke secured the buggy and hopped down. He loped around and held out his hand to assist her to the ground. Their eyes met. Electricity zapped between them.

The second her feet touched the pavement, he pulled his hand back and the moment was gone. He gestured for her to walk in front of him. She bit back a sigh, her heart heavy with things she could not have. The glass doors whooshed open as they approached, and they entered the air-conditioned lobby. Within a minute, they had the room number.

"Of course." The receptionist smiled. "Deputy US Marshal Bender explained that you were coming to see Mr. Stevens and that we should let you in, as you were the closest thing to a relative he had."

She didn't know how she managed to keep her face smooth. To say they were close to relatives was quite a stretch. Although, the man's entire family was gone. What if he really had no one else?

If something happened to *Mamm*, she'd still have Abigail, Rhoda and Betty. She also had Caleb and the hope he might awaken one day. What did Terry have? Sympathy clogged her throat. She'd done the right thing in coming to see him.

They piled into the elevator and took it to the second floor. The air between them nearly shimmered with emotion. All the things she refused to say hovered on her tongue. She pressed her lips together to guard against the temptation to blurt them out.

When the door slid open, her pulse thrummed in her ears. Still, she said nothing. At the door to Terry's room, she knocked, then waited, holding her breath. Inside, a man called out for her to enter. The weak voice lacked its typical arrogance, but she knew it at once. Letting out her breath, she opened the door and entered the room, conscious of Zeke's warmth at her back.

Terry Stevens glanced at her and swallowed. Emotion flared in his eyes briefly before he looked away. She wasn't discouraged. He'd been through so much. And he had to learn how to make it through without his parents. That hurt. She knew from experience how deep that kind of pain went.

"Terry," she greeted him, keeping her voice neutral. "The— I was told you wished to see me."

She didn't want to mention the police, or anything that hinted of the murder of his mother and father.

He nodded. Then he didn't say anything. She didn't break the silence. The muscles in his jaw worked. Finally, he spoke.

"Yeah. Molly." He paused and swallowed. "They—the police—told me my mom and dad are gone."

She blinked to keep her eyes dry. Tears wouldn't help him.

"They also said the man who killed them tried to kill you."

"He did."

A single tear spilled down Terry's pale cheek. His complexion turned gray. "I'm so sorry. This is all my fault. I had bought drugs from him several years ago. If I hadn't, he wouldn't have targeted my house. Or you."

She moved closer to the bed. "Terry, the fact that you bought drugs from him once did not give him permission to harm your family." He stilled. *Gut.* He was listening. "You did not ask for this. I didn't, either."

Slowly, she reached out and touched his arm. He jerked, but didn't pull away. "I wanted to thank you."

"Thank me? What for?"

"When Scott Davis ran after me, you tackled him and took the bullet he planned to use on me. You gave me time to get away. Because of you, I found help and my family was moved to safety. So, thank you."

"I haven't always been nice to you. I made fun of you, because you were Amish and had to clean homes. I'm sorry for that."

With effort, he lifted his gaze to her. "I'm very glad you're alive. The only thing I've ever been proud of in my life is that I kept my former dealer from killing you."

His words were rough, but she smiled at him.

She glanced around the room. It was a typical hospital room. Sterile with no personal touches. "Terry, is there anything you need? I still have a key to your home. I can bring you something to do so you're not too bored."

He shook his head. "That's kind. But I don't want to be a bother."

She smiled. "It's no bother. I can go to your *haus* today. Then tomorrow I'll have someone bring me here to drop it off."

"If you really don't mind? There's a stack of business books on the kitchen counter. I've been taking summer classes and don't want to get behind."

Her respect for him rose a notch. Not only had he apologized, but he was also trying to improve himself. She had to admire that.

"I can bring them."

She said goodbye and departed. In the hall, Zeke caught hold of her hand. "Hey. Are you sure you want to do this?"

She focused on his words, determined to ignore the tingling warmth of their connected hands. "*Ja.* It's the right thing to do. He's all alone, Zeke, and has so much guilt. If I can help him, I will."

"But the danger—"

"Is gone. Your brother shot Scott Davis. He's dead and can no longer hurt me."

"The ringleader is still out there."

She shrugged. "*Ja.* But according to Jeff, he canceled the contract for my death. Why would he *cumme* after me now?"

He didn't respond for a full thirty seconds.

She could see him struggling with her logic. Finally, he tugged her hand, urging her to continue walking. "If you're sure, we can—"

She stopped again and gently removed her hand from his. "I'm going to drop you off at your *haus*, then I'll do it. No reason you can't get some work done. There are repairs you need to make to your home, ain't so?"

"*Ja*, but I said I'd go with you."

"You did. I can do this part by myself." She needed to begin the process of rebuilding her independence. "I'll be fine. I'll go to his *haus*, get the books he wants, then return home. Tomorrow, I'll get a ride here and give him the books. Then I will be finished with this painful part of my life."

He began to walk. She kept pace. They rode the elevator in silence. In fact, neither of them spoke again until they were in the buggy and journeying away from the hospital.

"I want to make a request."

She glanced at him, cautious. "What?"

"I have no right to ask, but as your friend, I would like to go with you tomorrow when you bring Terry the books."

She should say no. That would be the smart

thing to do. But she couldn't respond to the warmth in his words with coldness. "I would like that. Are you free at two in the afternoon?"

He nodded, a smile molding his handsome mouth. She caught her breath and faced forward. "*Gut*. Two it is."

They arrived at his *haus* without any issues. It felt wonderful *gut* not to fret about whether or not someone would be waiting to kill them around the next corner. She might be able to sleep through the night. Once she thought about it, though, she wasn't looking forward to spending a night in her family home alone. It would be *gut* to have *Mamm* and her sisters back.

"Are you sure you don't want me to go with you?" Zeke paused halfway out of the buggy. He looked funny, suspended there.

"*Nee*. Look around. You have enough to do without that. I'll be fine."

He turned his head to survey the storm wreckage. A loud, huffy sigh left him. Tree branches were everywhere. Although his *haus* hadn't sustained any damage, the barn roof would require some repair. And she rather suspected he was determined to rebuild his farrier wagon. Her heart ached when she remembered the sound it made as Scott Davis deliberately destroyed it.

Hopefully, he'd find the time to create another one.

"Okay. If you're sure, I'll see you tomorrow at two."

She nodded. He sauntered away from her. She watched him disappear into the barn. A shiver crackled up her spine. The feeling that she should have asked him to accompany her creeping over her.

Enough.

The danger was gone. She was a grown woman. She'd be fine going to the *haus* and grabbing a few books. It would take her a few minutes, then she could return home and lock the doors. Life had sure changed. Until recently, she didn't bother with locking doors. Most people in the community didn't worry about it.

She'd never go to bed again without securing all the doors and windows.

Shaking her head at her foolish thoughts, she flicked her wrists, urging the mare to trot. She looked back two minutes later. She couldn't see Zeke's place anymore. But she also couldn't see any signs of danger. She rotated her shoulders, working out the stress gathered there. There was nothing to worry about. Just like she'd told Zeke.

She might need to remind herself of that a few times.

She slowed the mare at the Stevenses' *haus*. For all her talk that she would be fine, and she could do this alone, she couldn't deny she was uneasy at the thought of returning inside the *haus* where Nancy had died. Less than a week ago, a family lived here. Now, only Terry survived. She doubted he'd want to live here after his traumatic experience. She would not want to, either.

She had to do this. Only then could she be free of her fear.

Clenching her hands on the reins, she directed the mare to walk up to the *haus*. The crime scene tape had been removed, but she saw one small ribbon of yellow had been left behind, probably torn off in the storm.

That's when she recalled the key. She'd forgotten to grab it before she headed over. She bit her lip, thinking. Nancy used to hide a spare key near the flower garden. Climbing down from the buggy, she headed toward the garden.

She checked between the stones around the small flower garden in the front of the *haus*. The key was still there. Wiping it on her apron, she approached the *haus*. At first, she walked toward the back entrance, like she normally did. It hit her then that it looked similar to when she'd *cumme* to clean Tuesday morning. No cars in the driveway. Apparently, no one home but her.

That day hadn't ended well. She steeled herself and tried the back door. The key slid in, but when she tried to push the door open, it wouldn't budge. She'd have to use the front door. Shaking off her unease, she walked to the other door and slipped the key into the lock. Letting the door swing open. She took a minute to peer into the *haus* before taking a deep breath and stepping into the front hallway. It didn't look any different. She headed to the kitchen.

She almost took off her boots out of habit, then chided herself. She'd be inside less than a minute. And the police had left a bit of a mess behind. The small amount of dirt dragged in by her boots would hardly signify.

She looked at the door, and immediately saw why it wouldn't open. The doorknob had been damaged and the door had been boarded shut. Had it been injured by a bullet, or the storm? She shuddered as the image of Scott Davis charging after her took over her mind for a moment. She shook her head and looked once more at the broken doorknob. No one would be able to go in or out that door until it was fixed.

The pile of textbooks lay on the counter exactly where Terry had told her they'd be. Great. She would take them and tomorrow drop them off. Then she'd be done with this chapter in her life.

She picked them up and started to spin around to march to the front door and return home.

The floor creaked behind her. It was her only warning.

An arm snaked around her throat, and another caught her elbow.

Bile surged in her throat as he breathed on the side of her face.

"I can't believe you came back here. But now I can finish what I started and leave."

She froze, terror paralyzing her mind.

FIFTEEN

She knew that voice.

Molly struggled, throwing her elbows back and kicking her boots, aiming to slam her heels against his shins or to stomp on his toes. She missed. He chuckled in her ear.

"It's no use. I'm stronger than you are. The less you struggle, the easier it will be."

She'd told Zeke the ringleader wouldn't come after her. Not only was she wrong, but she had also known the man out to kill her all along.

Just like she knew he had no intention of letting her go. He'd never intended to let her live. And the concept of an "easy death" didn't thrill her. She increased her efforts. One of her elbows sank into his stomach.

"Oof!" A poof of air hit the side of her face. She had knocked the breath out of him. Literally. Yanking her body from his grasp, she stumbled forward two steps then spun around, intent on finding a way out. When she came face-to-face with her attacker she froze.

She was right. Sick horror filled her as she stared into the familiar face.

Frank Stevens. "You're dead."

He wasn't smiling or chuckling anymore. His large hand rubbed his side where she had elbowed him, a fierce scowl on his face.

"Obviously, I am not. The same cannot be said of you."

She believed him. A man capable of killing his wife and attempting to kill his only son would have no problem killing the Amish girl cleaning his *haus* weekly. They had only spoken two or three times. She never expected something like this. He had never crossed her mind as a suspect.

The police had thought of him, she recalled. But his "death" had put an end to that. They wouldn't *cumme* looking for her here.

The front door? *Nee.* That was hopeless. She would never make it past him.

He took a step in her direction, his hands reaching out to grab her. She was out of time. Wheeling around, she took off toward the back of the *haus*. He was only two steps behind her. If he'd had a gun in his hand, she would have been dead already. She reached the dining room doorway and grasped the small, wooden tiered shelf with glass panels Nancy had used to store her fancy knick-knacks, and Molly gave it a hard yank, dodging out of the way as it crashed to the ground behind her. Shards splintered and skittered across the hardwood floor.

Frank yelled. She heard a note of pain in his voice. Some of the glass might have cut him. She had neither the time nor the inclination to feel sympathy for her would-be murderer. Only relief that she might have slowed him down.

She heard a squeak as a door opened and metal clanged. Her blood froze in her veins. He had taken a gun from his gun safe. She was sure of it. Now he was angry and armed.

Clomping through the room, she deliberately pounded a few steps down the hall leading to the den and the master bedroom. She pushed the door to the den open.

When she heard his footsteps approach, she ducked inside the door leading down to the basement and stood on the top step in the dark, breathing hard. He strode past her and his steps paused at the den. When she heard him enter, she sagged. He had taken the bait.

She turned the knob. It was locked. She was trapped by her own cleverness.

Now what?

She had to try to find a way out from the basement. She hated basements.

Waving her hands at her side, she flinched when her knuckles bounced off the railing. Had he heard that? She paused. No running toward her, so maybe not. She slid her fingers down the railing and took it step by step until her feet touched the hard cement floor.

Some light filtered in through a small window to the left side of the basement. She made her way to the window, keeping her hands in front of her just in case she didn't see something in her path. When she arrived, she reached up, hoping she could open the window and climb out.

It would not budge.

Spinning around, she forced the panic away. She needed to find a way out. A long string brushed her face. The light. She pulled on it and a tiny circle of illumination burst into the room.

Footsteps stopped at the door.

Terrified, her head whipped back and forth, trying to find hiding places. There was an old freezer unit under the stairs. She remembered Nancy's excitement when their new upright freezer had arrived last month. She had cleaned this one out and had planned to move it to the garage to use for a storage locker.

Hurrying toward it, she opened the lid. It was empty.

She hurried to turn the light off, then returned to the freezer, grabbing a washcloth from a clothes basket on her way over. Trying to move silently, Molly climbed into the freezer. She ducked down into, folding the washcloth and propping it into a corner to leave an inch to breathe. It wouldn't do any good to escape if she suffocated to death inside an old freezer.

Shuddering, she hunkered down and waited.

Above her the door opened and heavy footsteps started down the stairs.

Would she leave the *haus* alive?

The steps continued. Blood pulsed in her ears, nearly drowning the sound of his approach. A sudden sliver of light bloomed in the crack at the opening. She knew what had happened. He had turned on the light.

It would only be a moment before he figured out where she was hiding. She bit her knuckles to keep from crying out. Instead, she prayed, hoping *Gott* would hear her, asking for one last chance. And if this were her final moment alive, she prayed He would see justice was done and her family protected.

And He would be with Zeke. She knew Zeke would take her death personally. In the past few days, they had become friends, even closer than friends.

The door flipped open with enough force to shake the large appliance and send the washcloth tumbling over the edge. Frank glared down at her.

"I don't have time for this, girl. I need to leave before the cops figure it out and come after me."

She cringed away, pressing her back against the side of the freezer. It was useless, she knew, but she was not about to let him shoot her without trying to escape. His hands reached for her and she kicked out at him. He retaliated with a heavy fist to her jaw. Briefly, stars exploded in her mind.

When he reached again, his meaty hands painful on her arms, she yelled and wiggled.

It wouldn't be enough.

* * *

"Zeke! Are you home?" Micah's voice yelled in through the back door.

"Ja." Zeke sauntered out of the back bedroom and met his brother and Steve in the hall. "What's wrong?"

He read the distress in the crinkles at the corner of his brother's eyes. Something must have happened to Molly.

"Where's Molly?" Steve broke in. "She's not at her house."

He shook his head. He wanted to scream at them to give him information. "She said she wanted to go back to the Stevenses' *haus* today. Terry had asked her to bring him something. She felt bad about disliking him and agreed."

He didn't like the horrified look dawning on the faces of his brother and brother-in-law. "Micah! What's going on? I thought she was out of danger."

"Come on. I will explain in the car."

The three men dashed to the SUV and hopped in. Zeke didn't bother with the seat belt. He slid to the middle of the back seat and sat on the edge, propping his arms on the headrests. His gaze flashed between the two law enforcement officers sitting in the front. His shoulders were so tight, he felt like a rubber band stretched to the breaking point.

Micah put on the lights without the siren and floored it. Zeke clutched the headrests so he would not fall back. He needed to know what danger was after his girl now.

He didn't even flinch as his mind acknowledged what his heart had been feeling. It had only been a few days, but he already knew he loved Molly Schultz in a way he had never expected to love anyone.

He wasn't about to lose her now.

"Dental records came in," Micah finally began. "The body found in Frank Stevens's car wasn't him."

"Wasn't him," Zeke replied, astonished. "He faked his own death?"

"We're not absolutely sure, but it looks like it. We did get some more information on the man who killed the officers at the safe house. It turns out, he's Frank's cousin. He's bad news, and has an arrest record a mile long. He's never going to see the outside world again after this, but Frank is still out there."

"He might be dead," Zeke began.

"Might. But I doubt it. I think he needed to disappear."

"What about the kid that shot Terry and Nancy?"

Steve twisted in his seat to look at him. "Scott Davis. He's dead. But he was probably working for Frank. I haven't figured out how they're connected yet, but my gut says it is only a matter of time until we do. And I also think a man who'd shoot his own wife would go after Molly."

A minute later, they arrived at the Stevenses' *haus*. An unfamiliar car sat in front of the garage, the motor still running.

With an exclamation, Micah slammed his SUV into Park and fled the vehicle, running for the door. Steve and Zeke were only a step behind. The door was unlocked. They stormed into the *haus*. At first, he did not see anything. Then Zeke stepped forward and something crunched beneath his feet.

The men cast simultaneous glances at the floor. Glass littered the area. Looking to the side, a wooden shelving unit filled with figures was smashed on its side. Zeke felt all the air leave his lungs. Were they too late?

A sharp feminine cry galvanized them into

action. They flew to the door leading to the basement. Micah flung it open, his gun at the ready. "Stay here."

He and Steve bounded down the stairs, leaping over the last five.

Zeke had always been one to follow the rules. Until the woman he loved was in danger. He dashed after them, hurtling down the stairs so fast inertia kept him moving at the bottom until he smacked into the wall.

Bouncing back, he turned. A little light was on, casting a small circle of light. The string was still swaying, telling him it had been pulled on recently.

Under the stairs, a large chest freezer stood open, empty except for the young woman standing in the middle of it, struggling with a tall man. Frank Stevens. Micah grabbed hold of him and practically ripped him away from Molly.

"Frank Stevens, down on the ground. You are under arrest."

Rather than complying, Frank yanked a gun out of his pocket and aimed it at Molly.

Zeke yelled as he threw himself in front of her, protecting her with his body. He heard the sounds of struggle behind him. The gun went off, missing Molly. A sharp sting along Zeke's side made him gasp, but he ignored it otherwise. All of his attention was on the lovely woman gazing up at him. Dirt crusted her face and dress. She had a bruise glowing on her face. Had he struck her? Other than that, she appeared fine.

Gratitude surged through him and he uttered a prayer of thanksgiving. He had not been too late to save her.

Micah and Steve had Frank cuffed and read him his rights.

"Do you have her?" Micah asked him.

"*Ja.* You go. Take care of him."

They marched Frank, who was growling a steady stream of invectives and idle threats, up the stairs. For a moment, they listened to the voices dwindling. Then he turned back to her. She was shivering.

Probably shock. He glanced around and saw some laundry sitting on the dryer. He grabbed a towel and sniffed it. It was clean and dry. He wrapped it around her shoulders. His side twinged and he grimaced. He didn't think he had been hurt bad, but he'd get it checked out as soon as he assured himself that Molly was well.

"*Cumme.* Let's get you out of there."

With his assistance, she managed to climb over the edge and stand on the floor. She swayed slightly.

"Are you dizzy?"

She shook her head. "My legs are cramped, but I'm *gut.*" She lifted her gaze and stared at him with haunted eyes. They pierced him straight through to his heart. "He was going to kill me. I don't know why. I don't understand any of it."

"It's a wonderful scary story, Molly. I have not heard all of it. But my brother might have the answers soon."

They made their way up the stairs. She went to the kitchen door, stepping over the glass. "I knocked this over to stall him."

"*Gut* thinking." He felt his legs tremble. His head grew muzzy.

"Your brother and Steve are leaving with Frank. It is *gut* I have my family buggy here. I can drive you home."

"I might need to go to the hospital first."

She whirled to face him, eyes flaring wide.

He could barely get the words out to tell her what he meant, but he had to tell her. Maybe it hadn't been a *gut* idea to wait so long.

SIXTEEN

"I'm sorry, Molly." Zeke's lips twitched in a faint smile, but pain furrowed his brow. "I think I've been shot."

Her hands flew to her mouth. She had not seen any signs of a wound on him. Even as she tried to deny his words, his eyes latched onto the dark stain spreading along the side of his blue shirt.

Blood.

Zeke slid down the wall, his legs crumpling beneath him. The moment he hit the floor, his eyes rolled back in his head and he toppled over, hitting the floor with a harsh thump. Dust billowed up around his head, covering his beard.

"Zeke!" Molly screamed his name and rushed to his side. Was he breathing? She glanced at his chest, sobbing out her relief when it rose and fell. Although the blood-stain spreading across his side terrified her. She patted his face with her hands, ignoring the stinging in her palms, attempting to bring him around. He remained unconscious. Visions of her father and Aaron dying and Caleb in a coma threatened to overwhelm her. She refused to give in. This man had risked everything for her. She would be strong for him.

She loved him. She wouldn't lose him now, not if she could help it.

But what could she do? She had no medical training. She didn't know if he was just unconscious or if he was seriously injured. Maybe Micah was still there. She ran to the window and peered out into the late afternoon, scanning the driveway.

She was too late. Micah had already departed, Frank stuffed into the back of his SUV. And why not? As far as he knew, they were both fine and he was free to go.

If only Zeke had told them he had been shot before he'd gone out the door. His brother would never have left him. If she had learned anything about the Bender brothers, they didn't let each other down in times of trouble.

She didn't have time for this nonsense. She

needed to get him to the hospital immediately. If only the phones were working again, she could have called for an ambulance. Unfortunately, that was out of the question. For the first time in her life, she wished she owned a cell phone. *Nee*, there was no one else to help her. She was on her own with an unconscious and possibly dying man.

But she wasn't on her own. Closing her eyes, Molly reached down into the depths of her soul for that little spark of faith that had been growing over the past few days. She held on to it for all she was worth. *Dear Lord. Please help me. Grant me the strength to get this man into the buggy so I could bring him to the hospital. Please, keep him alive.*

Zeke moaned. Molly ran back to him and dropped beside him. She leaned forward, so close, her forehead almost touched his, and framed his beloved face with her trembling hands. His warm skin assured her he was still with her.

"Open your eyes, Zeke. I have to get you to the hospital." She repeated her plea two more times before she finally got a response. Another deep growl rumbled from him. She held her breath and watched. His eyes open slowly and he squinted up at her.

"Hard to breathe," he rasped.

"I'm sorry. I need you to help me get you standing. Please. Help me."

He raised an arm, silently asking for her assistance. She stood and grabbed hold of his hand, pulling him off the floor while he pushed himself back up the wall. They were both sweating profusely by the time Zeke was on his feet. She dragged his left arm across her shoulders and held tight to his wrist. Her opposite arm snaked around his waist. She pulled tight, anchoring him to her side. He shook, and his steps were unsteady, but bit by bit, they left the *haus*. A couple of times, they came near to tripping and falling back to the ground. Zeke's flailing arm caught her in the ear once, and her once-crisp white prayer *kapp* landed on the ground, dusty and limp.

She ignored it. It wasn't important, not while he needed her help. His breathing concerned her. The wheezing noises accompanying each inhale seemed unnaturally loud to her sensitive ears. She had no idea of how much time passed before they arrived at the buggy. It might have been fifteen minutes or thirty. All she knew was he was still alive and conscious, although she didn't think he would remain conscious for long.

She would never know how she managed to get him into the buggy, but she did. She took a few minutes to make sure the horse was bridled and ready and then she hopped up and flicked the reins. The buggy lurched forward.

Zeke grunted and slipped lower in his seat.

He was unconscious again.

Molly ordered the horse faster, pushing their speed as much as she could safely.

She winced every time they hit a pothole or whenever the buggy lurched due to a rapid turn. The roads were littered with downed branches. A couple of roads later, she had to take a back way due to a power line blocking her path. As she turned, the buggy jolted. She cast a concerned glance at Zeke. He did not make another sound. It was all she could do not to give in to the fear clawing at her throat. The only way she could stave it off was through a constant litany of prayer. Her mind was too foggy with her emotions and chaotic thoughts to actually formulate any kind of real communication with God. All she could manage was to ask him for help again and again. The words *help me* dropped from her lips in a steady beat keeping time with the clopping of the mare's hooves.

Finally, the hospital came into view. The carport was empty. She sighed in gratitude that she wouldn't have to fight her way through. She didn't have it in her to drag him out of the buggy and carry him into the hospital.

She drove the horse under the carport and then reined the mare in. She jumped out of the buggy, landing on her injured leg and nearly stumbling. Righting herself, she half ran, half limped through the sliding double doors and burst into the hospital lobby. The woman behind the reception desk gasped, no doubt shocked by Molly's wild appearance, and jumped to her feet.

"My friend has been shot!" Molly choked out. She could hardly get her breath to make the words coherent. "He's unconscious."

She did not need to say another word. The efficient hospital staff flew into a whirlwind of motion. In less than a minute, a team stood at the buggy gently extricating Zeke's prone form from it. Molly couldn't take it any longer. The tears she had been holding in dripped down her face and off her chin. The gurney holding Zeke's body whisked past her and disappeared deep into the emergency room.

"Are you family?" The receptionist's kind voice broke into her thoughts.

Molly shook her head. "*Nee.* He is a friend. A very dear friend."

She could hardly tell them he was a man she loved with all her heart. She had not even told Zeke that. In fact, even if he lived, she had no indication that he would welcome such knowledge. Did he love her? She knew they had developed a connection. She recalled how he had held her hand. All the times their eyes met. But there had been no promises. No talking of the future. And Zeke's past held as much pain, if not more, as her own.

Enough. That didn't matter. Whether he returned her feelings or not was irrelevant. All that mattered was that he lived. She could be satisfied with that, even if she couldn't have him for herself. At least he would still be in the world with her.

The receptionist gave her a sympathetic look. "I'm sorry. Only family is allowed in the emergency room. You will have to wait out here."

Molly grimaced and nodded. She had expected as much. With a halfhearted wave, she made her way toward the waiting area. As she went past a picture with a reflective surface, she halted and stared at her image in it. She had completely forgotten that she did not even have a prayer *kapp* on. She was a rumpled mess. The braids wound around her head were frizzy and frayed. Her once-pristine dress was covered with dark splotches. Zeke's blood. She shivered.

Turning away from the disturbing picture, she crossed her arms around herself and stumbled over to a chair. She dropped into the chair, her mind numb with grief and anguish.

A phone rang at the counter.

The hospital phones were working!

Suddenly, she sat straight in her chair. Zeke's family didn't know he was at the hospital. He needed his family with him. Regardless of whether they had to remain out here or could enter the emergency room, they needed to be here, and he shouldn't be alone while fighting for his life.

The best way to contact them would be

through Steve, Joss's husband. After all, he was a police sergeant, and would have the means to contact the rest of the family. Additionally, he knew what had been going on, so he would be able to explain the situation. If the hospital phones were working, hopefully the phones at the police station were, too.

Heaving herself to her feet, she made her way to the reception desk again. She was bone weary but resolute. The woman smiled up at her, her penciled brows raised inquiringly. "Yes? How can I help you?"

"I would like to contact my friend's family."

The woman pursed her lips, no doubt wondering how she would contact an Amish family.

"His sister is married to a policeman at the Sutter Springs Police Department. Sergeant Steve Beck. Maybe I could call him?"

Although the woman blinked, she maintained her professional smile and agreed. She dialed the number and asked for Sergeant Beck. "Hold, please."

She handed the cordless phone across the desk to Molly. She took the phone and held it to her ear. "Hello?" Her voice quavered.

"Molly?" Steve barked. "Is that you? What's wrong—are you hurt?"

Hearing a familiar voice nearly undid her. She pressed her lips together, holding in her distress. After a moment, she spoke. "I'm not hurt, but Zeke is. We are at the hospital. He was shot—"

"You hold on, Molly. We're coming. Hold on."

She couldn't feel her fingers, she had held the phone so tight. When she heard him disconnect, she handed the phone back to the woman and somehow managed to return to her seat before collapsing into it.

Over the next hour, Zeke's family trickled in. Joss arrived first. She had taken the time to find someone to watch the *kinder* and had picked up Zeke's parents and his brother Gideon. Steve arrived next. He kissed his wife and enfolded her in his arms. Micah's wife, Lissa, stormed in, her face pale.

"I dropped Shelby and Liam off with my friend Ginger," she announced. "Any word on Zeke?"

All eyes turned to Molly. Before she could talk, the doors whooshed open again and Micah burst into the room. By now, the receptionist's eyes were so wide, they looked ready to pop out. It probably seemed odd, this collection of Amish, *Englisch* and officers all waiting on news regarding their Amish relative.

"Molly, I shouldn't have left so quick," Micah started. "Did someone else attack you?"

The whole family bristled. Tension rippled in the quiet space.

"*Nee*, you did what you had to do. I didn't know it when you left… He'd never said… Sometime during the scuffle at the *haus*, he'd been shot."

Collectively, they sucked in shocked breaths.

Steve released Joss and stepped forward. "Did you call an ambulance? I didn't hear a call come through."

She shook her head, flushing. "The landline phones were still down. Neither Zeke nor I had a cell phone. I dragged him to the buggy and drove him in."

Edith Bender pushed her way through her *kinder* and their spouses. When she reached Molly, she bent to wrap her arms around her.

Molly buried her face in the woman's shoulder. She had no tears left, but she was exhausted.

"*Denke*, Molly Schultz, for saving my son."

She was a fraud. Zeke's family gathered around her, all of them kind and admiring. As if she were a wonderful *gut* Amish woman.

She wasn't, though. Her faith, while growing, wasn't as strong as it should be. She'd let herself doubt *Gott*'s love for so long. What kind of example was that?

All her hopes to tell Zeke she loved him dwindled as the truth of her own unworthiness swelled inside her and filled her soul. Zeke Bender deserved a woman who was whole and authentic. One who would raise his *kinder* up right. A woman unlike herself.

Ten minutes later, when the members of his family were all gathered in little groups, talking quietly, she excused herself and walked out the doors to go home where she belonged.

Every time Zeke opened his eyes, someone different stood next to his bed.

Mamm and *Daed*.

Gideon.

Joss.

Micah.

Steve there once, too. But never Molly. He knew hospital rules limited the number of visitors and only allowed family in. The urgency to know she was well itched under his skin like a pound of fleas had been poured in the narrow hospital bed with him. Not only that, but every time he opened his mouth to ask the person at his side how she was, the medicine pumping through his system pulled him under before he could hear the answer.

The next time he awakened, Micah was at his side again. Zeke opened his mouth, but Micah didn't let him get the words out.

"She's fine, Zeke." He shook his head, awe coloring his voice. "That woman got you to the buggy and brought you to the hospital by herself. The whole family is amazed. And grateful. She saved your life."

Zeke swallowed. She was fine. And she had gotten him here.

"You didn't tell me you were shot."

He heard the gentle reprimand and reproach. "I'm sorry. I didn't deliberately mislead you. This might sound ridiculous, but I didn't even realize I had been shot until you left. I heard your car start and realized that my side felt like it was on fire. I looked down and my hand was covered with my own blood. I know it doesn't make any sense."

Micah nodded, understanding dawning on his face. "It was the adrenaline. That kind of rush will do that to you. Look, I'm just glad you're going to be okay. When I got Steve's call that you had been shot and were at the hospital in the emergency room, all I could think was that I was going to lose another brother. I just don't know if I could've taken that."

Which reminded him that they still had not heard from Isaiah. Not in person. But Zeke had hopes that someday his brother would come home. He didn't care if Isaiah was Amish or *Englisch*. None of them did. At this point, they just wanted him back.

Lifting his head a couple of inches off the pillow, Zeke looked around the room. "This isn't the emergency room."

"You're a bit behind the times, bruh. That was yesterday. You were in surgery for four hours. Thankfully, the bullet didn't nick any vital organs. You lost a lot of blood, though, and needed a transfusion."

That felt weird, knowing someone else's blood was flowing through his veins. "Who donated?"

"Gideon and Joss were matches, so they

both donated. I offered, but I was not compatible."

"Denke."

"Don't mention it. Anyway, you were in recovery for a few hours and then they brought you here, to your own room, a few hours ago. If the doctors are happy about your progress, you can go home tomorrow."

Frowning, he began to shake his head.

Micah cut him off. "Don't shake your head at me. You almost died. You're going to follow the orders and stay until the doctor tells you that you are allowed to leave."

He nodded. But his mind would not stay off Molly. The urgency grew inside him. "Molly? Where is she? Will the doctors let her *cumme* and visit for a few minutes?"

This time, Micah hesitated.

"What? What aren't you telling me?"

His older brother huffed an annoyed breath. "Fine. Since you won't let it go. She's not here."

Narrowing his eyes, Zeke surveyed his brother's blank countenance. "I thought you said she brought me here, ain't so?"

"Yes. She did. But that was yesterday. While we were all waiting for you to come out of surgery, she left."

Alarm rose up inside him. "Left! Have you checked on her? Is she safe? Was she hurt yesterday?"

Wait a minute. What was he doing lying here while the woman he loved was at home, possibly hurt or scared? He struggled to sit up, intent on swinging himself out of the hospital bed and finding a ride to Molly.

"Easy." Micah gently pressed him back down. "We don't know where she is. Her family isn't home yet. I swung by the house this morning. They should be back tomorrow afternoon, though, and I plan to swing by on my way home."

Hours. He had to wait hours until he could see her. The pain in his chest had nothing to do with the bullet hole in his side. She had not returned to see him.

"Are you sure she's out of danger?"

Micah nodded. "Frank confessed to everything. He had hired Davis to murder his wife and make it look like a robbery gone bad. Only, Terry came home early. He'd bought drugs off Davis in the past and thought his former dealer was there to shake him down. He wasn't supposed to be injured."

Shaking his head, Zeke stared at his older

brother in horror. "He planned his wife's murder? That's—that's— I have no words."

His own wife had betrayed his family to save hers, but he would never have wanted her dead. To even consider such a thing astonished and appalled him to his core.

"It's bad," Micah agreed. "Apparently, she'd begun to suspect that he was involved with something dirty, but hadn't completely figured out that he was skimming funds from her family business, in which he worked. He was heavily in debt, and they had a prenup that said if they divorced, she retained what she brought into the marriage. Which pretty much amounted to everything they owned. She'd visited a lawyer the day before and had him served with divorce papers. It was only a matter of time."

He had never been so glad to be apart from the *Englisch* world. The simple Amish life was hard, but in so many ways, it was easier on the body and soul. Now all he wanted was to settle down. It struck him then. He wanted to marry again. He wanted to spend his life with Molly at his side and raise a family.

Her current absence, though, did not bode well for his plans. If she had been the one in the hospital, he would have returned and practically lived in the waiting room until he could see her and reassure himself that she would be well.

He needed to know if he had any chance with her. Even if her answer was no, he had to know.

"Wait for me before you go to her *haus*, Micah." He met his brother's gaze. Not a muscle shifted in Micah's expression, but Zeke felt the sudden compassion emanating from him.

"Maybe you should give her time."

"Maybe so. But if I wait, she will have time to convince herself against us. I need to see her today."

One way or another, he needed to know if they had a future together.

SEVENTEEN

It was nearly five the next day by the time the doctor cleared Zeke to leave, giving him a small stack of papers containing instructions for caring for his wound and information regarding the antibiotics and painkillers the doctor had prescribed. He would wait to fill pain medication. If he could survive on over-the-counter drugs, that would be his preference.

Micah met him at the door. Zeke hopped out of the wheelchair as quickly as his injury allowed. Being confined like that, knowing someone else controlled your destination, went against the grain. But he didn't complain, knowing it was policy. The hospital staff had their jobs to do.

Stiffly, he climbed into the passenger seat of Micah's shiny black SUV, grateful that his brother, while hovering anxiously near his side, allowed him the dignity of getting in without help. He bit back a groan when he twisted to yank the seat belt across his torso and fasten it.

"You good?" Micah asked, his voice quiet.

"*Ja.* I'm fine." It might not have been the absolute truth, but he didn't know how else to respond. The condition of his heart was something no one, not even his oldest brother, could help him with. It was up to him, *Gott* and Molly to ease his sadness.

Micah sauntered around the front and got into the driver's seat. He regaled Zeke with the latest antics of his *kinder* while they drove along the winding roads. Zeke appreciated his brother's attempts to distract him, although they weren't completely successful. It was equally difficult to pay attention to the scenery. Normally, he enjoyed traveling and seeing the wonders of *Gott*'s world.

Today, the sun was shining, there was a light breeze, and the air was heavy with the aroma of flowers. But he could not take his mind off Molly, constantly wondering why she left the hospital before seeing him.

The car ride to the Schultz farm seemed to last forever, and at the same time, it was over all too soon. Zeke had tried to compose what he planned to say to Molly in his mind, but it never seemed right. He didn't want to sound too rehearsed. On the other hand, he feared he might stumble over his words and embarrass himself. He had always been deliberate and taken care with his words, yet when it mattered most, his mind froze.

"Take it easy," Micah urged. "You'll be fine."

"*Ach*. She did not want to see me at the hospital. I might have made a mistake. Maybe I shouldn't have *cumme* here."

"You did not make a mistake. Listen, I went through a rough time with Lissa. I said I needed space, but then got so nervous that I had waited too long that I almost didn't go back to her. I could have missed out on marrying the woman who completes me and the children who fill my days with joy."

Zeke sighed. "Lissa let you into her life. I don't know if Molly will. It could be that she doesn't feel the same way for me."

Now he was becoming maudlin. Firming his jaw, he pushed the door open. "I'll never know if I don't talk with her."

Easing himself out of the vehicle, he closed the door behind him, made his way up the walk to the back door and knocked. The family had returned home an hour ago. Micah had called in to the police department and checked on their status before leaving the hospital. The officer who had driven them home had just returned to the station. Hopefully, Molly had returned home, too.

His palms were wet. Wiping them on his trousers, he lifted his hand and rapped his knuckles against the windowpane. Then he stood back, clasping his hands behind him, swaying slightly on his heels while he waited. Soon, the door began to open. He stopped moving and straightened his posture.

Betty smiled at him. "*Gut* afternoon, Zeke."

He smiled back. The *kind* was pure sunshine. "*Gut* afternoon, Betty. I'm glad you're home."

"*Ja.* Me, too. *Mamm* was sad and worried about Molly. I didn't like it."

Ah, the candor of the very young.

"I understand. Is Molly home?"

She nodded. "*Ja.* She is out in the back field, looking for some vegetables to have with dinner. Are you staying to eat?"

He flushed and shifted his weight. "I'm not sure yet."

"I hope you do. Molly's been moping around here since we got home. I think she missed you."

He hoped so. "I'll go talk to her now, *ja*?"

She smiled, retreating back inside the *haus*. Indistinct murmurs filtered through the closed door. She was talking to her *mamm*. Probably telling her he might be eating with them.

He spun on his heel, momentarily forgetting to be careful of his injury. Wincing, he slowed his steps and headed back toward the vegetable garden. Micah raised his brows. Zeke pointed to the backyard and shrugged. Micah nodded and returned to typing on his phone. If Zeke had to guess, Micah was probably texting with Lissa, giving her a play-by-play of what was going on.

Rounding the barn, he saw her, standing motionless with her back to him, in the midst of the garden, her empty hands hanging at her side staring at the ground. The sorrow in her stance broke his heart. As he watched, a shudder ran down the length of her back. Then another. If she turned to him now, he would see tears tracking down her cheeks.

The temptation to leave and allow her to

cry in private halted his steps. But what if this was his only chance? And what if he were the cause of her tears? He could not leave her in her sorrow. Not unless she told him to go. If that happened, his heart would break, but he would never force his presence where it wasn't wanted.

Gathering his courage, Zeke approached her. When he was ten feet away, he stopped again. From here, he could hear the breathy sobs.

"Molly?"

She stiffened. The sobs ceased instantly. In fact, for a moment, it looked as if she had stopped breathing altogether. Then slowly, slowly, she rotated around and stared at him with shocked red eyes, her cheeks wet with the evidence of her grief.

Now he would discover if he were welcome or not.

She could not believe what her eyes were telling her. Zeke was here, standing right in front of her. Immediately, joy and trepidation simultaneously swallowed her. She really hadn't known if he would come after her. Part of her had expected he might feel relieved to have her gone. After all, they had met under duress. And even though they both showed evidence of feeling the same attraction, it was possible that it was the situation that caused their feelings of closeness and not any real affection on his part.

"Why did you leave?" She barely recognized the husky murmur of Zeke's voice. A wealth of emotion shivered in the deep tones. "I came out of surgery and everyone was there. Everyone but you."

She swallowed. How could she explain the heartrending feelings she had weathered over the past forty-eight hours?

"I didn't want to leave. I desperately wanted to see you, to make sure you would live. But I thought it would be less painful if I left."

His brow furrowed. "Less painful for who? Every time I woke up, I asked where you were. Unfortunately, I would fall asleep before I could hear the answer. When Micah told me you left, I didn't know what to think."

Molly rubbed her face with her hands and was shocked to find her cheeks were still wet. Her face flushed.

"Zeke." She halted, unsure how to explain. But she had to try. "I got scared. I saw your family, all of them standing there talking. Your family is so strong in their faith. You know how much I have struggled. I shoved *Gott* out of my life when tragedy struck. You know that's not how we are supposed to do it. Shouldn't that have been when I turn to my faith and rely on it the most? And then I thought of you and how you didn't lose your faith when tragedy struck you. I felt like I wasn't worthy."

Zeke snorted. Shocked, her eyes widened as her mouth dropped open. That was not a sound she had ever heard him make before.

"Of course, my faith faltered when my wife was murdered. That's natural. We all question at times. Do you think my parents didn't question why they suffered when my sister disappeared? Or why Isaiah has been gone for over a decade?"

Shrugging helplessly, she shook her head. "I didn't think about it."

"My family, by the way, thinks you are amazing. My mother and my brothers can't stop talking about how you lifted me into the buggy and drove me to the hospital. My father keeps telling me a special woman like you is a gift, and I would be a fool to let you walk out of my life without a fight. I happen to agree with him. A very smart man, my *daed*."

That surprised a laugh out of her. She had never had someone tell her she was a gift before. The sorrow that had clung to her since she left the hospital began to dissipate.

"You don't know me that well. Before this week, it's been years since we had seen each other. I might not be as special as you think."

He chuckled, shaking his head. His bangs flopped over his forehead. Her fingers itched to reach up and brush them aside. She clenched her fists and buried them in the folds of her skirt.

"Not likely." He examined her with gentle eyes. "Molly, I know we don't know each other well. I'm not asking for a commitment. Not right now. All I am asking is a chance to court you."

She bit her lip. She wanted to say yes. But she was scared to believe, to hope.

He must have seen her hesitation. "Please. I know it's early. But I won't abandon you. I know it's soon, but I love you. No amount of time will change that."

Tears spurted to her eyes. "I knew when

Frank had me, I knew I loved you. But I feel it's too soon."

He stepped closer and lifted one warm hand to run the backs of his fingers down her cheek. "Then we will take it slow. We'll walk out together, learn about each other, and when the time is right, we will make the next step."

Marriage. He wanted to marry her, but was willing to wait on her. Her heart swelled. For so long, she had refused to allow herself to dream or imagine a life beyond what she already had. Marriage and *kinder* seemed *verboten*—forbiddenfto her.

"Zeke, you know I was injured in that accident. I survived, but I didn't do it without scars."

She held her breath.

"I'm not surprised," he said. "Scars don't bother me. They are part of life. You're strong, caring, vibrant and brave. That matters more than your physical appearance."

"I'm worried I may not be able to have *boppli* of my own because of the accident. That's why I stopped going to the singings."

He smiled and touched her cheek. "I love you. I've always known that *boppli* are a gift. They are never guaranteed. But our love is a gift, too. One I never expected to have. As long as we're together, I'll be happy."

She sighed, one weight off her shoulders. There was one more thing she needed to know before she could claim the dream hanging so tantalizingly close.

"There's my family. My *mamm* and my sisters. I can never leave my family. They depend on me."

He nodded, a tender smile overtaking his face. "We would make it work. I don't care where we live once we're married. As long as we're together. They're *welkum* wherever we decide to build our home."

He had already made up his mind, she realized. He was willing to wait so she would be comfortable. She laughed, feeling like she had sprung a latch on a cage and walked into the sunlight. She would walk out with him. And in a few weeks or months, when he asked her to be his wife, she'd say yes.

His eyes sparkled at her laugh. Leaning forward, he kissed her, his lips pressing softly against hers. Warmth spiraled through her.

She couldn't wait to step into the future and see what *Gott* had in store for them.

EPILOGUE

Two years later

"Are you ready?" Zeke asked.

Molly stepped back from the kitchen sink and dried her hands on the dish towel sitting on the counter. She aimed a grin at the handsome man standing in the doorway. Zeke grinned back at her, his bright blue eyes shining with joy. Her breath caught in her throat and for a moment, she had to swallow back the tears threatening. Two years of marriage hadn't erased her wonder that this strong man was hers. Forever.

Her hand smoothed her lavender dress with its matching apron, feeling the slight swell under her hand. He'd also made her dream of becoming a mother one day a reality. Only the day before, she'd been assured of the presence of new life with the floating sensation of bubbles. It was a sensation she'd never forget.

"Wait a moment." She padded into the next room. *Mamm* sat in front of the fire, mending one of Rhoda's dresses, her glasses slipping down her nose. There was an air of contentment around the older woman these days. *"Mamm?"*

Her mother lowered her sewing to her lap and smiled at her oldest daughter.

"Ja?"

"Zeke's here. We're going now. Please remind Betty and Rhoda to feed the chickens and the horse when they get home from school."

"I will. We'll be fine." She made a shooing motion at her oldest daughter.

Molly hurried back toward her husband. She braced one hand on his shoulder and slipped her feet into the warm boots next to the door before grabbing the stiff black bonnet hanging on a hook and shoving it down over her prayer *kapp*. Then she took her black cloak out of his hands and swirled it over her shoulders. A fluffy layer of snow had fallen during the morning while she'd worked, and the brisk November wind continued to blow it about it sudden gusts.

Winter was definitely on its way. There was something breathtaking about the shimmer of the first soft snowflakes of the season.

She turned back to her husband and smiled. "All set."

He swooped down and pressed a quick kiss to her lips. She grinned wider. *"Denke."*

"I couldn't help myself. It's been six hours since I last kissed you."

Chuckling at her silly husband, she allowed him to guide her down the slippery steps and walk and into the buggy. Dear Zeke. He took such wonderful *gut* care of her and her family. True to his promise to her, her *mamm* and sisters had come to live with them after they married. Abigail was no longer with them. She'd married two weeks ago and had moved into her husband's *haus*. She was only a few miles down the road, though, so Molly saw her on a regular basis.

The only wrinkle in her joy was her brother, who remained in his coma. The doctors couldn't tell them when he'd wake up. He was breathing on his own. His vitals were stable. They had to feed him through a tube, but when she visited him every week, he looked like he was merely sleeping.

She'd also done something she'd never thought she'd have the courage to do. A week before she and Zeke exchanged vows, Molly had sat down and written Collin Vincent in prison, offering her forgiveness. She hadn't heard back from him, but she didn't need to. Her heart was at peace. She had done everything she could to make sure she was right with *Gott* before starting her new life.

"Molly? Are you well?"

Shaking herself out of her morose thoughts, she smiled at her husband. Today they'd check to make sure their *boppli* was well. Normally, Amish women didn't go to the clinic for prenatal visits. However, she'd been so sick that Zeke had grown concerned. He'd asked Levi about it, and their friend had told them it would be acceptable for them to visit the doctor to have Molly and the *boppli* checked out. Molly had agreed, although she wasn't worried. The fluttering in her belly was a frequent reminder that her little one was thriving.

Zeke gently wove her arm through his and guided her down the steps and across the driveway to the car waiting for them. They'd be returning after dark, so he'd hired a driver for the trip into town.

A young man around her age waited for them behind the steering wheel, reading on his cell phone. When he saw them approach, he set the device aside, an open smile warming his face. He opened the door and stepped out of the car, then opened the back door for Molly. "Afternoon, folks. My name's Andy. Go ahead and get comfortable. Please buckle in, too."

She settled into the back seat and clicked on her seat belt before relaxing as the flow of heat from the vents washed over her. It was the one advantage, in her opinion, that motor vehicles possessed over the horse and buggy they normally traveled in. She didn't care for all the fancy gadgets, saw no reason for the speed on most days. And the radio, which their current driver had set a little louder than necessary, was a distraction from the people in the vehicle with her. She couldn't hear the conversation up front between Zeke and the young man behind the wheel.

She put these thoughts aside and turned to peer out the window, intent on spending the next few moments in quiet contemplation and prayer, praising *Gott* for all His many blessings. Her hand rubbed her stomach. *Soon, little one. We'll meet soon.*

The car lurched, dragging her from her introspection. Startled, Molly jerked her head to the front. Zeke and the driver were both laughing and shaking their heads. After a moment, she joined in. Apparently, their young driver had gotten so distracted by their conversation, he hadn't turned into the parking lot quick enough and his car wheel had collided with the curb. Yet another reason to prefer traveling by buggy.

Still, she was grateful for the ride and thanked him generously.

Zeke escorted her inside the clinic, keeping hold of her elbow so she didn't fall, and bade her to find a comfortable seat while he checked them in. He waited until she actually sat down before going to the counter. She chuckled. Dear Zeke. Always the protector. He would make a wonderful *gut* father. How could he not be? She couldn't imagine a better husband. Strong and gentle all at the same time.

A bubbling feeling in her stomach made

her smile. It was almost as though their *boppli* agreed with her.

Within a few moments, he had rejoined her and sat on her left side. Her normally calm husband was as skittish as a cat in a room full of rocking chairs. His right leg began to bounce. Slowly at first. That didn't last long. Soon, his leg was bouncing so rapidly her chair, and her entire body on top of the chair, began to vibrate slightly. Molly reached over and placed her hand on his knee, applying enough pressure that he got the message and ceased. He shifted in his seat and gripped her hand.

"It's *gut*, Zeke. I'm not worried. I've felt the *boppli* move all morning. He's fine."

He nodded. His posture relaxed. "*Ja*. I know you're right. But we're here, and we have taken up a spot in their schedule, so we'll keep it. It's the right thing to do."

They sat in comfortable silence, in tune with each other, until a nurse stepped out and called, "Molly Bender."

She grinned. It always brought her joy to hear her married name said aloud.

Together, they followed her back into one of the rooms. The nurse took Molly's vitals and asked some basic health questions. She typed the responses on a laptop, her nails clicking on the keyboard. Molly blinked. She didn't know how she'd manage with nails that long. Closing her laptop, the nurse prepped Molly for an ultrasound.

Ten minutes later, Molly and Zeke stared at the nurse practitioner blankly before turning to each other. Molly read her own shock in Zeke's face. Shock and joy. They didn't say a word. Just listened as the speaker continued to emit the sound of tiny heartbeats. Two sets of them.

"Twins. Oh, Zeke. We're having twins!" Tears gathered on her lashes and slid down her cheeks. For so long, she'd feared she'd never be able to have *kinder* of her own. And now the *Gut Gott* had blessed her with two at the same time. Her heart was full enough to burst.

Zeke opened his mouth, then shut it quickly, swallowing. He just nodded, his own eyes shiny and damp, then leaned in and touched his forehead to hers.

"Congratulations, Mom and Dad," the nurse practitioner said. "They both appear healthy. Make sure you're ready early. Twins often come before the due date."

She couldn't wait.

A few minutes later, they were ushered back to the waiting area, a small stack of papers clutched in Molly's hand. She couldn't stop grinning. No wonder the motion seemed so constant.

"I should have guessed," Zeke murmured as they walked out to the car. The driver saw them coming and waved. "Gideon and Joss are twins. I know such things are often common when there's a history in the family. It just never occurred to me."

"*Ja.* It never crossed my mind, either. I was so grateful to be having a *boppli*, I never thought beyond that."

Excitement zipped through her. Normally, Amish women didn't talk about pregnancy to others, so she wouldn't say anything to her sisters. *Mamm*, though, *mamm* would want to know. It would give her pleasure, so Molly would tell her.

She stopped suddenly, jerking her husband to a halt at her side. There was someone else she wanted to tell.

"Molly?" His brow furrowed in concern.

She smiled at him. He might be a little over-protective in the next few months. She could live with that.

"I want to stop by the hospital."

His concern melted into understanding. "You want to tell Caleb. We can do that, *ja*."

How she loved this man! He didn't scoff or tell her it would be a waste of time, that her brother was in a coma and wouldn't hear her. *Nee*. Not her man. He offered unconditional love and support. She was blessed, indeed.

As they approached the running vehicle, Andy looked up from his phone and waved. Zeke opened the back door, waiting for her to enter and get situated before shutting it firmly and hopping in to the front passenger seat.

"Hope everything went well." Andy shifted and hooked his arm over the seat, turning his body so he could look out the rear window and back up. "Am I driving you folks home now?"

Zeke shook his head. "Actually, if you have time, we'd like to swing by the hospital to visit my wife's brother for a few minutes."

Andy shrugged. "I have time. Nothing else on the schedule today. So I'm at your service."

She released the breath she'd been holding.

She'd feared he wouldn't be able to accommodate them, but now that worry had been removed.

When they arrived at the hospital, Andy drove under the carport to allow them to exit on dry ground. "I'll watch for you. Wait until I come to pick you up when you are ready to go home."

They thanked him and walked inside. Molly tightened her grip on Zeke's hand. The memory of the horrific trip to the emergency room two years ago had lost its hold on them over time, but it wasn't something she'd ever forget. She focused on the feel of his hand in hers to banish any lingering pain.

The nurses didn't even blink when they arrived to visit Caleb.

Once in the room, Zeke grabbed the chair leaning against the wall and brought it next to the bed. Molly thanked him and sat, aware of his presence always at her side. She drew strength from it as she gazed on the still face of her brother.

"Look at his eyes," Zeke whispered.

She looked at the closed lids. At first, she saw nothing. After a moment, she saw movement. His eyes were moving under the lids.

She waited a moment but sighed when the movement stopped and he didn't awaken.

"Hello, Caleb," she began. It no longer felt odd talking to him. In her heart, she hoped he could hear her and something she said would one day reach him and pull him out of his comatose state. "The family is well. I know it's not usually talked about, but Zeke and I decided you should know that you're going to be an *onkel*, Caleb. Not to one *boppli*, but two. We found out today. Caleb, I want you here when my twins are born. I want them to know their *onkel* Caleb. Please come back to us."

She looked away, blinking back tears. It had been more than three years since he'd gone into the coma. Surely, he'd come out of it soon.

"How are you going to handle twins?" a rusty, broken voice said. "What's happening?"

Her head whipped up. Caleb was staring at her, a confused look on his face. His gaze was slightly unfocused. Zeke rushed to the other side of the bed and pressed the button to call for assistance. Then he hurried back to her side, a teary grin on his face.

"Oh, Caleb!" She scrubbed at her eyes,

wanting them clear so she could see his face. "You're back!"

It would take time, she knew. Her brother had missed so much. But he was with them again.

He glanced at the man standing beside her, his eyes widening in recognition. Except the last time the men had seen each other, Zeke had still been single.

Happily, she slid her arm through Zeke's. "Caleb, I want to officially introduce my husband, Zeke Bender."

A tear slipped down Caleb's cheek. "Your husband."

He lifted a weak hand and offered it to his childhood friend. "*Welkum* to the family, Zeke. My sister couldn't have found a better man."

Molly reached out and took his other hand, while leaning her head on her husband's shoulder. *Gott* had given her a family and brought her brother back.

Her joy was complete.

* * * * *

If you enjoyed this book, don't miss the other heart-stopping Amish adventures from Dana R. Lynn's Amish Country Justice series:

Plain Target
Plain Retribution
Amish Christmas Abduction
Amish Country Ambush
Amish Christmas Emergency
Guarding the Amish Midwife
Hidden in Amish Country
Plain Refuge
Deadly Amish Reunion
Amish Country Threats
Covert Amish Investigation
Amish Christmas Escape
Amish Cradle Conspiracy
Her Secret Amish Past
Crime Scene Witness

*Available now from Love Inspired Suspense!
Find more great reads at
www.LoveInspired.com.*

Dear Reader,

I love writing books connected by family. This collection of stories revolving around the five Bender siblings has been especially fun, and sometimes challenging! Thank you for taking the time to read *Hidden Amish Target*, which tells the story of Zeke Bender.

Zeke is considered the quiet, reflective brother. He never does anything impulsively. Until he meets Molly Schultz, that is. Molly's life has her questioning her faith. I hope you enjoyed watching her reclaim her faith as they fell in love.

I love hearing from readers! You can find me on Facebook and Instagram or contact me at www.danarlynn.com. Sign up for my newsletter to get the latest book news and giveaway opportunities.

Blessings,
Dana R. Lynn